By the same author

Dear Michael, Dear Laura.

Geoffrey Hamilton

My Short Book of Tall Stories

BY

GEOFFREY HAMILTON

MAPLE
PUBLISHERS

1

My Short Book of Tall Stories

Author: Geoffrey Hamilton

Copyright © Geoffrey Hamilton (2023)

First Published in 2023

ISBN 978-1-915996-89-3 (Hardback)

Book cover design and Book layout by:
> White Magic Studios
> www.whitemagicstudios.co.uk

Published by:
> Maple Publishers
> Fairbourne Drive, Atterbury,
> Milton Keynes,
> MK10 9RG, UK
> www.maplepublishers.com

A CIP catalogue record for this title is available from the British Library.

Contents

COME BACK RACHEL

And I Looked, and behold a pale horse, and his name that sat on him was Death, and Hell followed with him.................. (St. John)

Mathew was 12 years old and fed up. He shivered for the umpteenth time and decided finally it was time to move. Taking his gaze, for a moment, from the figure some 35 yards or so to his right, he looked down from the top of the fence then jumped safely to the ground.

As the raw February air nipped his ears and fingertips, he drew his coat closer about him and looked again anxiously at the girl in the distance. The wind seemed to be getting colder and colder, stabbing icily into his face, and forcing his eyes to water as he stared.

Just as Mathew was about to shout for the fifth time, the girl turned in his direction and called to him "Come on Mathew, over here and help me". The voice was high and crackled with the cold, the owner being his 7-year-old cousin, Rachel. She was a tall child for her age but slim with long blonde hair that hung down to her shoulders almost covering the red scarf that was wrapped several times round her neck. Her black belted overcoat contrasted sharply with her pale but pretty face now furrowed in anticipation of a reply.

The reason for Mathew's anxiety was that Rachel was standing on the edge of a pond recently frozen over, but to Mathew, decidedly unsafe. He thought again of his mother's last words to him as he walked together with Rachel down the drive of her home "Don't forget, look after Rachel in the park and bring her home safely".

Mathew and his mother Eva had driven over from their home in Wimbledon today as they had done every Sunday afternoon since Mathew could remember, to visit his aunt Julie and cousin in Richmond. So it was to Richmond Park that the two children were bound with mum's parting words ringing reflectively in Mathews ears.

Without waiting for a reply, Rachel turned and walked further across the ice. "No, no, come back Rachel, come back" Mathew screamed as he raced towards his cousin. On reaching her he grabbed her arm and pulled her back to the edge of the pond. "You are an old misery Mathew Barnes, why don't you go home" said Rachel as she struggled free from his grasp. "I will, and I'll tell your mum what you're up to", he retorted. He turned and started running across the grass, assuring himself that this was possibly the best course of action to take. He was tired of looking after Rachel and would be glad to hand the responsibility over to someone older. He knew Julie would soon have Rachel off the ice without hesitation. In his haste, Mathew failed to see the tree root poking out of the ground. His left foot caught the root and sent him crashing to the ground, his head struck a small rock and he passed out. The sudden noise startled a group of pigeons in a nearby tree, they rose and flew across the deserted park to nestle elsewhere.

So engrossed was she, in edging across the ice, Rachel neither saw nor heard Mathews fall. Already though, the ice beneath her feet had started to crack.

Eva Barnes was a short, stout woman in her late forties. Her face betrayed the suffering endured at the hands of her egotistical and overbearing husband., until her eventual divorce. On the day her divorce became absolute Mathew was born and Eva's suffering began all over again.

The child inherited his father's looks and temperament. Eva inherited the debts. What she was denied in looks she made up for in a warm personality, tenacity, wisdom and the occasional help of her well-off sister and brother-in-law. So, twelve years on, Eva's efforts on behalf of her child had truly paid off in the shape of a boy well mannered, intelligent, thoughtful, and now, unfortunately, unconscious.

Eva's sister, Julie, or Jay as she was known, was a total contrast physically, being tall slim and strikingly attractive. Aged some five years younger than Eva, she sparkled in the company of men. She had an outgoing kindly nature and positively doted on her only child Rachel. It was to the latter that the sisters were referring on that cold but memorable Sunday afternoon when the singularly strange occurrence took place. They were seated in the living room where Julia was pouring tea for them both and telling Eva the events of a boring party of the night before. She stopped speaking and stared hard at a point somewhere between the fireplace and the door. "What is it, Jay?" ventured Eva fearing the worst – a spider, maybe? "I, I, don't know" replied Jay, turning swiftly to face Eva. "I could swear I saw Rachel standing by the door beckoning to me". She shook her head and carried on pouring the tea. "How odd" voiced Eva" and shivered imperceptibly. "It's turning quite chilly in here Jay" She went on, "Shall we light the fire now?" Jay nodded her head in agreement and the incident was forgotten.

The Rachel, however, standing by the door was not imaginary nor paradoxically was she the Rachel so adored by her mother. She was, however, beckoning.

The air grew sullen over Richmond Park and the east wind blew harder making the grass stand up straighter than the hair on an angry dogs back. The park was now truly empty except for one small girl, defying nature in the wake of discovery.

Rachel had progressed about ten feet from the bank of the pond when she stopped, turned, and scanned the undulating scenery for the fleeting figure of Mathew. She had tired of her game and without

Mathew's watchful anxiety her excitement had turned to boredom. Rachel decided to return home. At that moment however, the ice under her feet gave up its concrete existence and split wide open. A massive fifty-foot crack stretching the length of the pond opened like a giant frozen smile. Panic! Rachel tried to run but the ice was too slippery, she lost her balance and toppled backwards into the icy depths. As her small body hit the freezing water she called for her mother. The piercing screams of "Mummy, mummy", from those terrified baby lips rose high over the pond, over the hedgerows, over the trees but were heard by no one. The water claimed its victim and there was silence.

As if by a sign, the sky grew instantly darker, the wind whined and howled in a requiem of fury. Small animals scurried for cover in fear. Birds rose angrily, screeching and cawing from the trees. Then, from out of the splintered ice, rose a form, diaphanous at first, a vision of a huge white stallion, winged and horned with flaring nostrils blowing smoke and sulphur. The mighty steed left the now frothing water and took up a stance on the pond bank. Blazing colour then burst all around the animal, then, upon it's back there materialised a nigrescent figure. It was the apocalyptic Angel of Death. That legendary skeleton in hooded robes had risen seeking a soul! Death stretched a bony arm and pointed at the hole in the ice where Rachel had perished. Directly, a small ghostlike figure climbed out of the water and stood upon the ice. Then, walking over to the Vision, stopped, and looked up. Dressed only in a long white shift that flapped idly against her ankles, the spirit of Rachel looked into the face of Death and waited.

The game evolved many years ago, since the time of Abaddon, the King of the bottomless pit, ruler of the 4 Angels of the mighty river Euphrates. It was played only once in every decade. The rules were simple; the spirit must run to the one that loves them most, alert them to follow, then, without waiting, return to the scene of their demise and re-enter their human body. If the spirit returns AFTER the loved one, life would be restored. If, however, the spirit returns BEFORE the loved one, Death would be the victor. And since time began the demonic angel never returned empty handed.

All this the spirit Rachel perceived with equanimity. Her small face looked unquiveringly and fearlessly into the black voids that were the eyes of Death.

So, the scene was set – the contestant ready. The huge stallion ended the silent audience by rearing up on hind legs, then tossing its leonine head into the air and bellowing through jagged teeth, its mouth dripping black saliva. The voice of Death thundered down to the spirit "GO" then "NOW". Without further ado the ghost-girl was off and running, running hard, literally running for her life. With hair and gown blowing wildly she tore across the park towards the gates. As she neared the fence, Mathews prone figure came into view, he was lying stretched out, a dark patch bled from his temple staining the grass a deep red. She slowed her pace enough to see that the boy was still breathing, then picking up speed she was through the gates and on towards the house. Eventually she reached her goal. Passing effortlessly through the front door, through the living room door, she stopped and stood silently by the fireplace.

"See me, see me" she pleaded mentally as she stared at her living mother. Julie's eyes met Rachel's and she froze.

Was it really her daughter standing there by the door in a thin white gown beckoning her to follow? Julie's eyes said yes, but her mind said no. She turned back to her sister for whom she was pouring the tea and tried to forget the incident. She could not. Even after lighting the gas fire the memory haunted her. Feeling Rachel's presence, seeing her, was it perhaps an omen or a presentiment of danger? Julie decided to go to the park. So, fifteen minutes after Julie first saw the spirit Rachel, the two sisters were on their way to the park in Eva's car.

During the drive Julie's anxiety grew, every fibre in her body told her to hurry, hurry. Her nerves became taut. "For God's sake Eva, can't you go any faster?" she snapped suddenly. "Steady on Jay, calm down" responded Eva, looking at Julie through hurt eyes. "We don't even know if Rachel IS in trouble". Julie reacted with fury "God that's rich, how typical of you, always looking on the bright side. Well get this Eva, Rachel IS in trouble and I'm worried sick, so let's get there fast". Eva bit her lip and said nothing. The rest of the journey was spent in silence except for the tap tapping of Julie's long manicured fingernails on the dashboard as she stared out of the car window.

Rachel's spirit could do no more, she must go on with the game; Death had ordered it. She had to run to the one that loves her most had alerted her, and now she must run back. The spirit girl turned reluctantly from the fireplace and began to run back. Tears were streaming down her pale elfin face. "She didn't understand" she wailed through motionless lips, and on she ran.

By the time spirit Rachel had reached the park gates she was ready for the inevitable. As she looked over her shoulder for the last time, she saw the car and hope sprang once more. The car slewed through the open entrance and came to a noisy stop. Julie and Eva leapt from the car and headed towards the pond. Halfway there they saw Mathew lying on the ground and stopped.

Kneeling beside him Eva called softly "Mathew, Mathew, can you hear me"? The boy moved his head from side to side "Come back Rachel, come back" he moaned deliriously. Eva laid his head gently back on the grass then rose to her feet, reached into her pocket, and removed her mobile phone and called for an ambulance.

Julie, meanwhile, had rushed over to the broken ice and discovered Rachel's body pale and lifeless beneath the water. "Oh Rachel, my darling, please don't be dead, please live" she screamed as she clutched the dripping frozen body to her breast. Julie left the water's edge and collapsed on the grass still holding Rachel's cold little body as she wailed hysterically. She stopped momentarily at the sound of Eva's voice. "I've phoned for an ambulance". Julie turned her head toward Eva, as she did so, the spirit Rachel slipped soundlessly back into her human body. Julie looked back at her little girl who suddenly started coughing as water dribbled from her mouth.

The ambulance arrived within minutes and the children were put safely into the back on two stretchers. After assuring the sisters that the children were now in safe hands. The attendant helped them into the back of the ambulance, then with sirens blaring they were headed for the hospital.

The park was now empty once more except for Death and his equine servant who pawed the ground anxious to be away. The Angel of Death surveyed the emptiness around him, then throwing his hooded satanic head back, laughed high into the wind, an eerie cackle so malevolent so evil it would turn warm blood to into ice. He dug his heels into the horse and away the pair galloped in pursuit of victory. Death was owed a life and Death never returned empty handed.

The ambulance raced through the cold damp streets of South London with lights flashing and siren blaring. They reached the hospital in a matter of minutes. As the ambulance turned off the road and through the hospital gates the journey had already ended for one small patient.

When Mathew's heart stopped beating, forever, the game was finally over for another decade.

⊷❖⊶

TWO OF A KIND

A huge July sun sat high in the cloudless blue sky over the city of New York. The temperature was in the 90's again for the third day running and getting used to it was still an effort mastered by few. But the weather was the last thing on Maxie's mind as he slowly replaced the telephone receiver gently on its cradle and stared silently at the dial. His motionless posture belied the sickening turmoil of his troubled mind.

Turning away from the telephone, he walked down the hallway of his sixth-floor apartment. The humidity of mid-summer bothered him as the stale heat circled like invisible steam causing his shirt to stick to his back in sweaty patches. Maxie turned at the sitting room doorway and paused resting his head against the open door. Perspiration trickled down his forehead mixing with the salt dried stains on his cheeks.

Surveying the room, Maxie's gaze came to rest on the wall by the mock Adam fireplace. His eyes followed the red line which started halfway down the wall and ended behind the body slumped against the polished baseboard. Tears welled up again in Maxie's eyes as his mind burnt with a paradox of fury and love. Why, why did you make me kill you his brain screamed out. Stumbling across the room Maxie collapsed on to the couch. Laying back, staring at the ceiling, he felt exhausted, drained. He closed his eyes and thought back to the first meeting with Angel Da Costa, three years ago.

He had just started as a bartender at 'Harry's Place' and within a month he was everybody's friend. Maxie advised, Maxie sympathized; serious one minute, witty the next. Confidences were kept, jokes were laughed at and at the end of the day he was, as they say, a regular guy, loved by all. But Maxie loved no one, or to put it another way, had no one to love. Until, that is, the day Angel walked into 'Harry's Place'. Maxie was smitten, it was love at first sight. Within a month Angel had moved into Maxie's apartment. Life was sublime. For two years anyway.

Out of the growing love Maxie had for Angel, there grew a jealousy that intensified with time. Out of this jealousy sprouted wings of possessiveness that flew in the face of reason. Maxie became paranoid. Angel became indifferent, then began going out with other men until Maxie found out and started threatening. Angel got the message and came to heel. Life returned to normal until the cataclysmic events of this morning.

Tilting his head forward, Maxie opened his eyes and gazed directly upon the outstretched figure of a uniformed soldier lying face down on the pink carpet. Another corpse. The sight brought a new fury to Maxie. Biting back saliva tasting of snake venom, he screamed out loud "Why Angel, why a goddamned soldier boy?" He brought his right hand up to wipe his brow and realized the gun was still in his hand. It was a small six-shot special, a mother-of-pearl handle led to a short snub-nosed barrel. The trigger guard was small and clung to his index finger like a ring. He shook his hand, but the gun stayed firm. Ignoring it, he wiped his forehead with the back of his hand. Still talking aloud, but softer now, Maxie went over the day's events. "I went to work this morning, I see Harry, he says George can't make it Friday, that's the other bartender Angel, so George gonna work today, have Friday as his rest day instead, you follow Maxie? Yeh, I says, I get you Harry, what's the beef? Well, he says if it's ok with you Maxie take your rest day today and show for Friday. I tell Harry no sweat, so 20 minutes later I'm back here at the apartment. That's it Angel, Gods honest, I wasn't spying on you".

Maxie's voice grew louder, his words came faster, as if reiteration strived for vindication. He continued the tirade. "I came into the room,

I saw you, saw both of you, the sonofabitch soldier boy had his arm around you, you were holding him, yea, holding him and smiling at his goddamned asshole face. I caught you and caught you good, I had the gun out and in my hand. I was mad now Angel, real mad, I had to punish you, you had to suffer like I was suffering. What was it you were going to say? Lies I expect, I don't care. Anyway, you must pay, no second chances". He jumped up from the couch and stabbed the air with his gun. " Bang, bang, bang, three for you and he got three". Maxie's emotions reached a climax and he subsided in uncontrollable crying. Throwing himself against Angels body, he gasped between sobs, "I'm sorry Angel, forgive me, I'm sorry, I'm sorry". Angels lifeless body slid slowly sideways to the floor, away from Maxie, as if in rejection.

Suddenly the doorbell was ringing, the sound filling the apartment. Maxie sat up, he stopped breathing. Someone was thumbing the doorbell. He waited, breathing out slowly. A splintering sound reached him.

The cops, thought Maxie, he turned and rose as two men entered the room, arms outstretched, gun barrels pointed at him. Maxie raised his arms in surrender, the small pistol still wedged on his index finger. The younger of the two detectives saw the gun flash, made the wrong assumption, and fired, the other cop followed suit in reflex. Maxie took both .38 slugs full in the chest. His feet left the floor as his body bucked and arched backwards like a thrown doll, his body came to rest on the floor under the window.

"Jesus Christ Steve, I thought the sonofabitch was goin' to waste us" gasped the nervous Detective. "No chance of that" said the senior man as he bent over the body, examining the gun. "Check those other two stiffs for ID Jim, while I call the Department". He left the room, made his call, and returned to the now silent sitting room. "Now then Jim, what have we got.

"Well sir, the soldier's name is Ralph da Costa, aged 38 and judging by his passport here (he handed it over to the Sergeant) he'd just got into town today from three years overseas. The other guy is called Angelo da Costa aged 31, here's his driver's license. I guess they were brothers. But why'd the punk blow 'em away then call us?" The crime weary older Detective pursed his lips and sighed. He looked from the documents to the three bodies. "I dunno' Jim, I really don't know".

THE SINNER MUST PAY

Harry and Felix both aged 45 had been friends for 40 years. They lived next door to each other, went to school together and played together, in fact did everything together. They were best friends, neither had any siblings so they were really like brothers.

The parting of the ways came when they left school, Harry to be an apprentice plumber and Felix to College then University to study medicine. They of course still saw each other from time to time to 'catch-up' on things.

Moving on a few years, Harry was now running his own plumbing business in Guildford, Surrey where he grew up. Felix on the other hand had become a successful GP in a medical centre in Petersfield Hampshire - not that far from Guildford. Their friendship continued, visiting each other, or dining out. They acted as Best Man at each other's wedding. Alas, neither had any children. So, life rolled on until the day Harry's business began to fail. He desperately needed cash to update and streamline the business, so he called up his best friend. Now Harry was always an easy going, funny, popular chap who had never asked help from anyone, until now. He really did not want to seek help, but he had too.

The telephone rang, Felix answered it. "Hello Felix, all well there?" Ah! Harry old chap, yes all well here, and you?" "Yes, yes, all good, look somethings come up, can we meet?" "Sure thing Harry come over". As much as Harry loved Felix, he accepted that he was 'old school' and strait laced, did everything by the book. He wasn't sure how he would react to his request for a loan. Anyway, he visited Felix the following morning and over coffee, blurted out his problems. Felix paused then asked, "How much?" It was Harry's turn to pause.

"£10,000 would put me on the right road. Of course, I'll pay you back every penny when the business picks up, I promise". Felix smiled, "Of course I'll help you; a promise IS a promise.

Six months later Harry's business had started to pick up, he even managed to open a second branch in nearby Woking. After 9 months Felix became a little twitchy but never mentioned payback. When 12 months since the loan came around Felix was not happy. He noticed how Harry and wife had gone on an expensive holiday abroad and how they had bought a new car. He decided to speak to Harry about the loan. He called at his office unannounced and spoke to Harry "Look old boy, can we talk?" Harry was a bit taken aback; he'd never seen Felix like this. Nevertheless, said "Sure please take a seat". He just came out with it "So when are you repaying the loan?". Harry sat back in his chair, "Soon Felix, honestly, sooner than you think, now I am really busy at the moment, I'll phone you". Felix left the office, he was furious, talk to me like that how dare he, he thought.

Two weeks later Felix phoned Harry, "Hello old chap, any chance we could meet up this morning?" "Sure Felix, where?" "Here in Petersfield, the Red Lion Inn carpark, say 11 o'clock?" "All sounds a bit MI5, but yes, see you there". "Cheers Harry, bye".

Felix was early. Sitting in his car he just kept repeating, it must be done, God help me, but it must be done. Harry arrived, parked his car got out and looked around. He spotted Felix's car and walked towards it; Felix signalled to him to get in. "Well, this is all a bit mysterious, what's up?". Felix turned to him, "I've got something to show you Harry, close your eyes". The moment he did Felix produced a syringe and injected Harry in the neck, he immediately went limp, his eyes just staring ahead.

"I'm sorry my friend but I have injected you with a paralytic drug, you cannot move but you can hear". Felix stared at Harry for a minute, then spoke.

"We have been friends for years, but lately you have stepped out of line, have gone too far". He started shouting, "Respect, honour, you have shown me none. Play by the rules of give and take, you have taken and not given". Harry's mouth started to open and close like a fish, "What's that b.b. but, is that what you're trying to say, but what, you're sorry, too late? A promise is a promise, you have sinned against me, and the sinner must pay". Felix then produced another syringe and injected Harry. His staring eyes closed, and he died.

Leaning across Harry he connected the seatbelt then his own. He started the car and drove out of the carpark turning right and headed for the nearby woods. Turning off the road he parked between the trees. It was silent, no one around. Felix opened the passenger door, undid the seatbelt, and dragged Harry's body deeper into the woods. He came to a 6ft by 3ft hole in the ground he had dug earlier. As he laid the body beside the hole Harry's eyes opened and his right arm twitched then moved upwards. Felix noticed, "Sorry Harry, not enough poison, ah well, doesn't matter now". He tipped the body into the hole then returned to his car to fetch a spade. After filling in the hole Felix drove home.

"Hello darling, said Edith, Felix's wife, just in time for lunch". "Jolly good my love, answered Felix, I'm starving". As they sat at the table eating Edith remarked "Oh, darling you haven't forgotten your birthday tomorrow?" "Of course not", replied Felix. "It's just that there are some cards for you", continued Edith. "Look, I think this one is from Harry, I recognise the writing". Felix slowly took the envelope, opened it and as he removed the card a cheque fell out it was for £30,000 made out to Felix.

He gasped, then opened the card and began reading. Dear Felix, you old stickler, Happy birthday, you are the best friend a man could have. I'm sorry about being cagey about the loan but I wanted to repay you on your birthday. I have upped the amount a bit to show you how grateful I am – you saved my life. All the best, Harry. Felix crumpled, my God what have I done, he thought. "Felix, you look dreadful, what's the matter?" said Edith as she patted him on the back. "Nothing dear, it's just what Harry wrote in the card, quite touching". "Fair enough darling, oh, by the way I've booked a table for us at the Red Lion Inn for dinner tomorrow night, is that ok?". "Yes, that's fine Edith, thank you". Just as she was leaving the room she turned, "Did you know the Red Lion has recently had cctv installed, cameras inside and out, so Miriam told me, state of the art apparently.

THE SECRET

Bill Wade was 78 years old and reasonably fit. His wife Enid had died a year previously, he couldn't live in the house they shared for 58 Happy years, so he sold up and moved to a town called Westbridge where he bought a small bungalow. But now he was alone, no friends or relatives nearby. He pretty much kept himself to himself. He did, however, have a sister called Janet but she lived in Canada, and they spoke on the telephone every so often. The last time they talked Janet suggested he got a dog, it would be like a companion so he wouldn't be alone, well, that's the way she put it. Billy said he would think about it. Two weeks or so later he decided – why not?

When he visited the Dog Rescue Centre, he was saddened to see how the dogs jumped up and down with pleading eyes when they saw him. He knew, they knew, why he was there. When Billy reached the last cage, he saw a little chihuahua sitting with his back to him, statue still. He knelt and said, "I want a friend, will YOU be my friend?". The dog turned slowly and looked at him, he put his paw between the bars.

After the form filling and 'home visit' Billy returned to the Centre to collect the little dog. When they got home, he sat on the sofa with the dog on his lap. "Now then, what am I going to call you, let me think". He pondered for a while. "Well, before I retired, I worked on the counter at a Bank, my title was a Bank Teller, I think I'll call you Teller, how does that sound?". The little dog gave a bark then licked Billy's hand. "Good, that's settled then". He gave Teller a hug then kissed him on the head. "Come on I'll show you your bed".

The next day the two of them went to the park. After a long walk round Billy sat down on a bench with Teller by his feet. Opposite was a similar bench with three men sitting, in deep conversation.

He strained to hear them. After a while Billy called out to Teller, "Come on boy time to go home".

Detective Inspector Jim Robson rushed to pick up the phone "Westbridge Police Station, can I help?" "Actually, I can help you," said the caller. "Go on, I'm listening". "Lacey & Co the jewellers, in the High Street, will be robbed tomorrow at 2pm". D.I Robson sat down. "How do you know?" "I heard them talking about it". "Them, how many?" "Three and they will be riding mopeds, and before you ask, I was in the park sitting on a bench, they were sitting opposite". Robson was intrigued. "I know the park, there's a wide path between the benches so how could you hear, also, didn't they notice you?" At this point the caller became a bit irritated. "Well, firstly I have good hearing and secondly I'm just an old man with a dog sitting on a bench with my head bowed". "I thank you for the information, now, what's your name?" The caller put the phone down.

Jim Robson couldn't believe his luck. Together with three other officers in 'plain clothes' he staked out the jewellers. At 2pm along came three mopeds with the riders wearing crash helmets. After a bit of a scuffle all three were arrested and taken Westbridge nick. Back in his office Jim called in his sergeant, "Any luck with that mystery caller Harry?" "No guv, phone box, no cctv, sorry". Jim sighed, "Just wanted to shake his hand".

About two weeks later Jim was out of the station when his mobile phone rang. "Robson, what's up?" "There's a bloke on the phone wants to talk to you, no name". "OK, put him through". "Hello Detective, go to 44 Bodley Street, the whole of the first floor is a cannabis farm, goodbye".

"Wait, wait, if you're right and can come up with other 'tip-offs', I'll pay you, what do you think?" There was a pause. "You'll pay me?" "Yes, replied Robson, but you must tell me your name and a time and place we can meet". Another pause. "My name is Billy Wade; I'll phone you later with a time and place to meet". The line went dead. Yes, thought Jim as he punched the air.

Billy was sitting on the sofa will Teller on his lap. "You will never guess what, but that policeman has offered to pay me if I come up with anymore 'tip-offs'". He looked at Teller who first yawned, then replied "Well, it's about time. I suppose he thinks it was you that heard those men talking about the robbery". "Of course I did Teller, I couldn't tell him it was my dog that wandered over and listened in, then wandered back and told me what they said, could I?" "No, fair enough replied Teller, and you told him about the cannabis farm?" "Yes, I did. Tell me what it was like living in that house Teller?" "Awful, terrible, my master used to kick and beat me, so I ran away and lived on the streets until the RSPCA rescued me". Billy was so moved by Teller's story. "Well, I'm not your master, I'm your friend". "Yes, said Teller, and I'm YOUR friend, tell that policeman you'll do it". Billy gulped. "Are you sure?" "Yes, I'm sure, I've been around criminals for a long time. I can sniff out all sorts of drugs and firearms. Also, with my acute hearing we can't go wrong". Billy was impressed, then said "We are not just friends, we are partners, but just one thing, let's keep the talking dog thing a secret". "Yes, said Teller, our secret".

THE SECRET EPISODE TWO

It was a cold day in Westbridge. In a High Street café, it was warm as Billy slowly drank a cup of coffee while he waited to meet D.I. Robson. He looked at his watch, 10am, he should be here soon. The café door opened and in walked the policeman. Billy stood up, this must be him he thought as the man approached, hand extended. "Jim Robson", he said. "Billy Wade", he replied. They shook hands then sat down. "So, you're the mysterious tipster". Billy blinked, "Don't know about that, would you like a coffee Mr. Robson?" "Call me Jim, no thanks I haven't got time, He pushed a brown envelope across the table, I wonder if you could help me?" Billy picked up the envelope, looked inside and saw the money, he looked at Jim "Fire away I'm listening". Jim cleared his throat, "There are these Serbians, three of 'em, importing and selling guns we know they're at it but can't get a warrant to search their warehouse, not enough evidence, we need 'eyes inside' if you get my drift". Billy his head down while he listened then looked up "I think I can help, leave it with me". "I knew I could rely on you, well, I must go". Both men stood up and shook hands. "I'll be in touch Jim".

It was busy that day, well it was busy every day at Heathrow Airport thought Billy. He stopped, bent down and picked up Teller. "Time for you to go into the old shoulder bag, don't want you getting stood on". Teller sat in the bag with just his head sticking out. "Have you ever been to an airport before, Teller?" "Er, no, silly question". "Yes, sorry about that – you haven't got a passport". They both laughed. Billy checked the overhead screens for incoming flights from Canada. "Ah, here it is, plane arrival on time". As he made his way to the arrivals barrier Tellers nose starting twitching as he sniffed the air. "He's dodgy – cannabis, the blonde girl – cocaine, man wearing red trainers – cannabis. "Shush Teller we're not on a case". "You're right, my bad, I'll cool it". Billy chuckled, "Going all American now, are we?" Again, they both laughed.

How their lives had changed since their first meeting at the shelter. Both had sad lonely unhappy lives, no purpose, no future. Now, after living, eating, and sleeping together, both had blossomed. They had listened to each other's life story, made each other laugh had a job they shared that paid cash. They had a future; they had a life.

Billy anxiously watched as the passengers neared the exit. "There she is, my sister Janet", he shouted at the shoulder-bag. People near him started to move away. Teller's head popped up "which woman is she?" Billy pointed, "The one wearing a red hat and coat". He started waving, she waved back.

When they all arrived back at the bungalow Billy sat down on the sofa next to Teller and Janet sat on the armchair. "You seem very perky these days", Janet commented. "Sorry, who are you talking to, me or the dog?". Laughter all round. "Before I show you round the house Janet, would you please come and sit on the coffee table and look at Teller", said Billy, seriously. She did. "Now what happens next might be a little scary". "Don't worry about me Billy, it takes a lot to scare me". "Fair enough, now ask Teller how he is". Janet smiled, "Ask the dog how he is?" "Yes yes, go on". "I think you're losing it Billy, anyway, how are you Teller?" "I'm very well Janet, how are you?" In a fit of terror Janet recoiled, slid backwards, and fell off the coffee table her legs sticking up in air. "Hmm, green knickers, that's something I can't unsee", remarked Teller. Billy rushed to help the now panting woman to her feet. She sat back down on the armchair. "He, he, can talk, a dog talking". "Sit tight Janet, I'll make us a nice cuppa while you talk to Teller". As Billy left the room, Teller shouted to him, "two sugars for me as usual". Janet stared at him with her mouth open. "It's alright love, I was joking". Janet smiled weakly.

When Billy returned with the tea tray, he was pleased to see the two of them chatting away like old friends.

Over lunch Billy told Janet all about Teller, and about the tipster business. Janet then admitted she hadn't been honest about her holiday visit to the UK, she had in fact decided to move back, permanently. "You're not cross with me, are you?" she asked. "No, the opposite, in fact why don't you live here with Teller and me, what do you say?" She reached across the table and caressed his hand, "thank you Billy, I would love to". "Well, that's settled then, oh, how would you like to join the business as well?" Janet was overcome. "Yes, I would love to, if that's alright with you Teller?" "It's ok with me, and welcome".

After explaining to the others, the details of the new job, the plan was now put into action later that afternoon.

The warehouse was situated in a remote area. The gates were not locked. Janet's job was to stay in the car in a layby about a quarter of a mile away as the lookout. Billy and Teller passed through the gates and approached the building, the entrance was on the corner. Teller waited round the side as Billy knocked on the door. He stood stooped carrying a walking stick. The door opened and a large bushy haired man stepped out. "What you want old man?". "It's my dog, he ran in here somewhere, I wondered if he had got into your warehouse". The man stared at him for a moment. "You stay, I look". He went in slamming the door shut. After a minute or so the door creaked open, "No dog, you go". With a bit of misdirection, Billy stepped back and pointed to the gates, "He came in through the bars, my eyesight is not very good, can you see him?" The man stepped forward away from the door. Teller rounded the corner and disappeared into the building.

The man looked around, "No dog, you go, NOW", he turned and went back inside. Billy left the yard and started walking back to his car. As he walked past the railings, he noticed how impossible it was for the police to stake-out the place, nowhere to park without being seen. It was then he heard Teller shrieking. With shaking hands he phoned Janet "Bring the car now, Teller's in trouble". Within a minute the car pulled up beside Billy and Janet got out, "What's happened?" "I think they've caught Teller, get down on the ground". They both lay flat out and peered through the bottom of the railings. The warehouse door opened and the big man kicked Teller out, "No come back". When the door shut Billy turned to Janet "Start the car, I'll get Teller". As he passed through the gates and ran to get Teller, he said to himself please be alive, please be alive. He knelt and picked up the little body, Teller's head turned and looked at Billy, "I got what we need". Billy hugged him as he ran towards to the car.

They went straight to the Vet's which was still open. He told them Teller had been attacked by a big dog. He was treated for broken ribs and bruising. He was kept in overnight and then allowed to return home.

Teller lay on the sofa with Billy beside him, Janet sat on the armchair. "Tell me what happened my friend". And he did. With pen and notepad Janet wrote it all down.

He entered the warehouse and hid behind some boxes and listened. One of the men was English so they all spoke in English, well, sort of. In 7 days there was to be a sale, the buyer would arrive at midnight. Teller paused for a moment due to the pain in his ribs. He continued. While the men talked he wandered round and saw wooden crates containing grenades in some, rifles in others. The lids lay nearby waiting to be attached. As he moved around, he bumped into one of the crates that had a toolbox balanced on top. The noise it made as it fell to the ground alerted the men, there was nowhere to hide.

They surrounded him, one tried to grab him round the throat, but he bit him between his finger and thumb and hung on. The man screamed in pain then punched Teller in the head, so he let go. The man then kicked him in the ribs, old memories of his past came flooding back. He stood up and limped towards the door. The three men just stood and watched – and laughed. 'Bushy hair' then ran forward, opened the door and kicked Teller out. Billy stroked Teller's head gently. "Well done my brave soldier, well done".

The next day Billy met with Jim again in the same café as before. He told him the date and time of the sale, the crates, and the weapons. Jim was amazed, "This is great info, well done".

At the appointed time armed police were parked up in a turning half a mile away from the warehouse – in both directions. As the buyer's van passed them, they waited 10 minutes, then the call 'Go-go-go went up. They blocked the road on both sides of the gates then entered the yard, weapons raised.

Billy and plus one was invited to D.I. Robson's promotion party. Billy shook Jim's hand warmly "Congratulations mate, I so pleased for you". "I wouldn't be here if it wasn't for you, Billy, I'll never forget that".

⚬⋯⊰⊱⋯⚬

THE BOOK

Telford Avenue in SW London is a lovely place to live or so thought 28-year-old Julian who lived there with his mother Edith. They shared a 3-bedroom maisonette that she and her late husband bought in 1973 for £10,000. Today worth £400,000. Julian could never afford to live in London. At the top of the road was Streatham Hill Station. Only a short journey into London where Julian, a professional dancer worked. His speciality was 'Tap', so when he got a part in '42nd Street, he was over the moon. He had worked on and off in various West End shows. One time he was in a show on a cruise ship. Julian was a very happy chap and living with his mother was a bonus. But things were about to change.

One day Julian was rehearsing in Tavistock Street. When the cast broke for lunch, he wandered down Charing Cross Road, he came to a small turning he'd never noticed before. Along this narrow street were several antique shops one being a bookshop. He entered. The owner, an elderly gentleman, nodded to Julian who asked, "Do you have any books on dancing?" The man pointed a bony finger at the lower two shelves of a bookcase. "Thank you, sir,". Julian had always been interested in dancers from the past. He got down on his knees to look along the bottom two shelves, running a finger along one shelf found nothing of interest. The final shelf, still nothing, except, right at the end he noticed a book tightly wedged. With some effort he managed to pull the book out. It had a dark red leather binding, no title on the cover nor the spine. That's odd he thought. He opened the book; the pages were old and brown and the edges uneven. Each page was numbered and handwritten in black ink they appeared to be poems in Latin. He suddenly felt a tingling in his hands and arms then a crinkly voice sounded in his head. "Welcome sire, so nice to see you". Julian was terrified. "Who are you?" he shouted. The shop owner looked up, "everything alright?" "Yes, I'm fine". The voice sounded again, "we will talk later – when you are alone". Julian shut the book and taking it to the counter asked how much. The man looked at the book without opening it "Well, it's been here for years - how about £2?" Julian paid and left the shop.

On the way home in the train, Julian couldn't stop thinking about the book or the voice. Am I having a mental breakdown he wondered, hearing voices in the head is a sure sign. He decided to throw the book out of the train window, but then he stopped, If I was to have a question-and-answer conversation, well, that would be something different.

He arrived home and on opening the front door caught the smell of Mum's beef bourguignon, lovely. Julian was in bed by 11pm. He opened the book. "Ah, you are alone, I will now tell you everything, my name is Merlin advisor to King Arthur of Camelot, the year is 1250. When Arthur was 20 years old in the year 1200, he pulled a magic sword from a stone when no others could. As a reward he was made King. The sword known as Excalibur is now missing. Later I discovered it was found 750 years later at the bottom of a lake in Bosnia and donated to the museum there. Now this is where you come in. The sword was stolen from the museum by a man called Ramiz Prazina, a Bosnian bad man" – "A gangster", Julian interjected. "If that is the term, Merlin continued, Prazina lives in London in a large castle" - 'Mansion' said Julian. "If you say so, your mission is to retrieve the sword". For the first time Julian relaxed and started to laugh, "oh, that's easy". "Well done sire". "wait, no, I was being sarcastic". "I fail to understand you sire". "What I mean is it's impossible, a house full of gangsters with guns – weapons I mean, it can't be done". "Oh sire, my apologies, I will give you magic powers". "Powers, Merlin?" "Yes, the book is your weapon".

Merlin continued, "each page in the book contains a magic spell. I will grant you three powers if you agree to the Mission. Meanwhile I

29

will let you think on it, we will talk again soon". Julian closed the book. The following day Julian started scrolling Google on his laptop. He found Ramiz Prazina, when he saw a picture of his house he gasped, it was huge, with steel gates and tall brick walls surrounding it.

After work Julian returned home. As they ate dinner, he told his mum everything about the book and Merlin. "That's nice dear, a bit different from dancing, how's the chicken chasseur?" Julian loved his mum's practical way of thinking. "It's lovely, but don't you think the Mission is a bit dangerous?" "Well not if you 'case the joint' first as the police would say". "No mum, the police would carry out surveillance on the property". "Well do that then son, take your dad's binoculars". Julian decided to accept the Mission.

Luckily, so to speak, dance rehearsals were cancelled for a week due to three dancers contracting covid. Back at home Julian opened the book. "I'll do it". "Do what sire?" "Oh sorry, I mean I will accept the Mission, Merlin". "Very good sire, I will now explain the magic powers".

The spell marked number 1 was the power over living things. No.2 the power over objects and No.3 Invisibility. As the spells in the book were written in Latin Julian must put his hand on each spell and repeat the text after Merlin. (He did this). Whenever he used a power, he must point with his outstretched arm and say just one word, but, he added, beware the spells only last a short while. Before they parted, Merlin said "If you wish to avail yourself of Prazina's coinage from his treasure chest, do so". Julian thought to himself I think he means rob his safe of cash. And why not?

After watching the house for two days, Julian was fairly sure how many people were there each day. At dinner on day two Julian told his mum he was 'going in' the next day "Can I use your car mum?" "Of course, you can dear, as long as I drive, now eat your fish". "No mum this is a solo mission". "Well, it will be son once you get out of the car, I've always wanted to be a getaway driver". They looked at each other and burst out laughing. "I love you mum".

At 2pm the Honda Jazz pulled up outside the back wall of the house. "Park nearby but out of sight mum, I'll call you". When the road was clear Julian, breathing heavily, pointed at the wall, and said 'open', brickwork fell away enough for him to enter. He walked slowly towards the back door. Hearing a noise, he knelt by a wheelie bin. A man, kitchen worker, came out leaving the back door open. He sat down on a nearby box and lit a cigarette. This is it thought Julian as he bent his arm, hand on chest saying invisible. Unseen he walked forward, passed the smoking man and through the open door into the kitchen, going forward then out of the far door into a corridor. He could hear laughing and talking but saw no one. Going into a large lounge and ignoring the people there, he surveyed the walls, no sword. He checked several other rooms, no sword. He ended up in a large foyer by the front door. He mounted the wide staircase, then at the top wondered which way to turn, left or right. It was then he realised the invisibility was wearing off, in a panic he knocked over a porcelain jardinière beside the top step. The moment it hit the floor with a crash Julian became visible. Two burley men appeared and ran toward the stairs. Julian was faced with several doors, he turned left and ran trying each one – locked – locked, the third one was open, he entered and closed the door. Suddenly he heard a key go in and the click as the door was locked. He looked around the room, it was Prazina's study and there on the wall was Excalibur, then removing a wall painting he found the safe, pointing he said open, the door swung open.

Taking a pillowcase from his back pocket (mums' idea) he filled it with bundles of £50 notes. Hearing voices outside Julian guessed he was about to be interrogated, tortured even. He heard the click as the door was unlocked, he froze in terror. A man entered the room slowly holding a gun, "Give me the sword he shouted". Julian, holding Excalibur in his right hand, raised his arm slowly as if to give it to the man, he spoke one word – blindness. The man panicked he dropped the gun and starting pawing at his eyes. Julian rushed to the door removed the key and lock the door from the inside. It bought him some time. He turned toward the left wall – 'open' the brickwork fell he was in a bathroom, on to the far wall – 'open' a bedroom on again another bedroom. This time he turned to face the door, as it swung open, he could hear the walls rebuilding. Turning left and down the corridor, he saw a back staircase at the bottom he turned and ran stopping only to use his mobile. "Mum meet me, same place". On hearing kitchen sounds ahead he knew where he was. Hearing footsteps Julian turned to see a tall man pointing a gun. He shouted, "Stand still or I shoot". Pointing, Julian said 'legs', the man crumbled to the floor the gun went flying. As he started to run, he heard a noise it was the man he was pulling himself toward the gun. Again, Julian pointed – arms, the man collapsed.

As Julian entered the kitchen, he was invisible, dodging the kitchen staff then through the back door he was out of the house and running like the wind. He reached the back wall shouting 'open'. Edith was in the car engine running, jumping in he shut the door and they were off. "Are you alright son, I see you got the sword". "Yes, mum I got it. He lay down and closed his eyes.

Arriving home Edith went into the kitchen to make them a cup of tea while Julian counted the money from the pillowcase. Returning to the dining room carrying two mugs of tea Edith was amazed to see the bundles of cash on the table. "How much is there dear?". "Well mum it adds up to £25,000".

There was one thing left for Julian to do. Sitting on his bed he opened the book. "How went the Mission sire?" "A total success Merlin, I have Excalibur". "Well done sire, well done". Julian then posed the question that had been bothering for a while. "Will you come to collect it?" "No replied Merlin, I am unable to cross time zones, but objects are. When I tell you, place your hand on spell number 4, I will quote the text and you will repeat, like before". Julian said he understood but asked what would happen next. Merlin replied, "A portal will open". "What's a portal?" Merlin went on to explain the spell would open a gateway between the zones, and Julian was to throw the sword into it. "One more thing sire, King Arthur has informed me that should your mission succeed, he will dub you an Honorary Knighthood. You will be known as Sir Julian a Lord of Camelot and a Knight of the Round Table". Julian was amazed. "Please thank his Majesty from me Merlin, I am truly grateful". "I will my Lord, now if you are ready, repeat after me spell number 4. Julian complied, seconds later a large hole appeared, he threw the sword and the hole closed.

Julian went back downstairs and sat beside his mum. "Everything alright dear?" "Yes mum, it's all over now". "Good, now remind me dear what show are you rehearsing for?" "You know what show". Edith patted him on the shoulder. "Tell me again". Julian shrugged his shoulders. "Ok, ok, It's the musical Camelot". Their laughter could be heard halfway down Telford Avenue.

BLACKPOOL

Lucy Simmons was washing up after lunch when the phone rang. "It's Chloe you're favourite cousin". Lucy laughed, "what a surprise". Chloe continued, "I know, I know, I'm about to make your wish come true". Intrigued, Lucy asked, "Wow, are about to send me a million pounds?" "No silly, I'm coming to visit you". Lucy paused for a moment. "When?" "Next week for a few days". She sat down then asked Chloe where she would be staying as stopping with her was not an option as things with her boyfriend are a bit fraught at the moment. No problem replied Chloe, "I'll stay in a B&B". Lucy suggested a place near the café where she worked. Chloe agreed, "I'll see you when I arrive then, bye love". Lucy said goodbye.

A few days later Lucy was busy in the café when in walked Chloe, she rushed to give her a hug, "good journey?" she asked. "Yes, fine". "Good, I've booked you a room at 'Seaview' and when I'm finished here, I'll come and see you.

Across the Blackpool beach the wind and rain were relentless. It was late September; the tide had ebbed far back leaving the sandy beach cold and empty except for the body of a woman lying face down. The figure of a dog-walker could be seen, distant at first, then closer. As he saw the woman, wet and bedraggled, he rushed and knelt beside her, he felt for a pulse, she was alive. God, he thought, she can only be about 20 years old. He phoned for an ambulance and the police. Taking off his outer coat he laid it across her like a blanket. An ambulance arrived, then DS Myles Clough. The woman had no identification on her. She received basic treatment at the scene then placed into the ambulance which drove away with sirens blaring. The police car followed behind.

Arriving at A&E the patient was rushed inside and treated. The police waited outside.

She was transferred to a side ward and examined by Dr Aziz. The girl never spoke a word, just stared wide eyed in shock. The doctor constantly assured her all was well, but still not a word. The examination caused some concern, DS Clough was asked to step in. He was shown bruising on the patient's neck and throat, he looked closer, "Looks like someone tried to strangle her, how old would you say she is?" "Somewhere between 18 and 25", said Dr Aziz. "I need to take her clothes", continued Clough.

Jane - as Myles Clough called her - was taken to the shower room, "let's get you cleaned up," said Aziz. She watched Jane as she undressed and stepped into the shower turned on the water and adjusted the temperature. No sign of mental issues there, she thought. She gathered up Jane's clothes and put them into a bag, then placed a towel and pyjamas on a chair and waited outside. After seeing Jane safely into bed, she handed the bag of clothes to Detective Clough.

Later, at Lytham Police Station, Clough's boss, Detective Inspector Chas Newton called his team together. On the evidence board was a photo and written below was 'Jane?' Tapping the picture, he said "Her clothes have gone to forensics, and as we have no ID, check for anyone reported missing, speak to the dog-walker again also check the incident book for any recent reports of domestics or acts of violence. Go to it lads".

While back in his office Chas got a frantic phone call from the hospital, a man had tried to strangle Jane. "Did you get him?". Chas asked. "Yes, we got him", came the reply. "I'm on my way". Grabbing his coat he shouted, "Clough, with me, now".

The two officers arrived at the hospital and went straight to the side ward, they could hear Jane howling in fear. Dr Aziz came out of the room to meet them, "I'm sorry he got away", she then turned to a man sitting on a chair holding his head, "Jim, could you?" He got up immediately and joined the group. "This is Jim from security". Chas looked at him and saw the blood on his nose. "I'm sorry sir, he was a big bloke, couldn't hold him". Chas patted him on the shoulder. "It's all right mate, you did your best, just give my Sergeant a description, OK?" Jim nodded. Chas turned to the doctor.

"How's Jane?" "Well, that's the odd thing, since she was attacked, she's started talking – sort of". Chas looked puzzled, "how so?" The doctor shrugged her shoulders, "she keeps repeating the words du sang partout, it means blood everywhere". Chas's eyes lit up, "she must be French, thanks doc".

On the way back to the car Chas's mobile rang, it was from the police station, the body of a female had been found in Derwent Woods by a group of ramblers. "I'll be there in 10, then turning to Myles, we got another one 'cept this one's dead".

Back at the Station Chas called the team together. "What's new lads?"

He was told forensics had found blood spots on the jeans and sweatshirt. He told them Jane was probably French so check abroad for missing females aged between 18-30. Before Chas and Myles left for the crime scene, he arranged for two uniformed officers to guard Jane's hospital ward.

They discovered the dead woman's name was Lucy Simmons aged 32.

Her address was 18 Denby Road, Blackpool. She had been stabbed to death. A subsequent search of the flat found evidence of blood in the lounge. Drugs were found in a tea caddy in the kitchen along with £2,000 in a biscuit tin. Fingerprints were found apart from Lucy's of a man called Jerome Parr, a small-time drug dealer. His photo was released to the Press.

Chas and Myles were good buddies both in and out of work. "Let's call it a day Myles, have an early night?" He then added, "why don't you and Pauline come for dinner, June's cooking a mean spagbol, say 1900hrs". Myles laughed, "Yes, we'll be there at 7pm".

Over dinner the two men discussed the case. Chas spoke first, "two incidents, one murder and a possible suspect and one attempted murder and no suspect". Myles replied, "here's a thought, why not show Parr's photo to that hospital security bloke, there might be a connection". "Good idea Myles. While all four were chatting, Chas's mobile rang, he answered, it was the night-desk sergeant. "Sorry guv thought you'd want to know; Jerome Parr's been arrested". "Thanks, Danny, see you in the morning", he then updated Myles.

The following morning as he entered the Police Station Chas was stopped by the Desk Sergeant. " A doctor Aziz phoned asked if you would come as soon as". He turned to go back out then said, "Tell DS Clough to follow up on Parr". "Will do guv".

As Chas looked at Jane through the ward window, he was pleased to see how much better she looked. Dr Aziz approached him, "Her name is Chloe Simmons aged 24, she lives in Rouen. Born in London but moved to France with the family when she was 12". Chas asked how she knew all this. "That's why I called you, Chloe is talking now". She pushed the door open, "come in I'm sure there are questions you want to ask her". He sat on a chair by the bed. Showing Chloe a photo of Parr he asked if this was the man who attacked her, she nodded. She went on to tell Chas, in her own words, what had happened. "I came over from France to visit my cousin Lucy in Blackpool and stayed in a B&B. When Lucy finished work, she came round to see me, it was then she told me how controlling Jerome was, she called him Jerry. I was not allowed in the flat unless he was there. The next day while we were on the North Pier Lucy said I could go her flat as Jerry was in Manchester for the day working. We were having a lovely time catching up when we heard the front door open, Lucy was in a panic and told me hide behind the sofa. He told Lucy he'd finished work early. It was when he spotted my overcoat on the armchair, he became enraged and started slapping Lucy's face". Chloe broke down, Dr Aziz handed her a tissue, she then continued. "He started shouting, Lucy shouted back, he then pulled her hair, and she slapped him. I peeped over the sofa and saw him take a flick-knife out of his pocket and stab Lucy in the chest three times. She fell, I tried to phone the police but was shaking so much I dropped my mobile, as I tried to pick it up, he heard me, I stood up and tried to run but he grabbed me round the throat.

He kept squeezing and squeezing". At this point Chloe put her hand round her throat as she relived the moment. She continued. "I put my hand in his pocket and brought the knife out then pressed the flick button, I stabbed him in the shoulder, he fell backwards over the sofa. I ran out of the flat and just kept running and running. That's all I remember".

Chas thanked her and wished her well. Before he left the hospital he showed Parr's photo to Jim the security guard, he confirmed it was Chloe's assailant.

The first thing Chas had to do on returning to the station was to interview Parr, but before that he had a sit-down with Myles and told him everything Chloe had said. "Come on Myles let's talk to the scumbag". Myles took a piece of paper from his pocket, "You might want to see this, Parr had it on him when he was searched". Chas looked at it then placed it in the case file he was holding.

They went down to the cell with Jock, a uniformed PC. Chas told Jock to handcuff Parr's hands behind not in front, "so much more uncomfortable". They entered the interview room; Parr's solicitor was already there. At the end of a 'no comment' interview the brief spoke, "If you're not going to charge my client then we are leaving". "We are charging him so you may leave now". He left. Parr stood up in a rage knocking his chair over as he did so. Chas ignored him and held up the paper that Myles had given him, "do you see this, it's a plane ticket that Lucy bought for France?" Parr smiled, "well she won't be going anywhere now, will she?" Jock spoke, "No, but you will", "Yeah, I know prison". "No, hospital". With that he raised his right leg and with his size 10 police issue boot kicked Parr in the genitals. The man fell screaming to the floor. Chas and Myles looked at each other then at Jock. "Resisting arrest, attacked me". The other two agreed, but Chas suggested he remove the handcuffs. "Just one thing, said Myles as he pointed at the wall camera" "Don't worry, said Jock, it's not working today, technical hitch".

Chloe left hospital and returned to the 'Seaview'. She explained things to Duggie, the owner, he was very upset; he knew Lucy very well. After buying a new mobile, Chloe phoned home saying she would be coming home very soon. She then joined Ben and Ruth, Lucy's parents, at 18 Denby Road after being told the flat was no longer a 'crime scene'. They gathered up Lucy's personal things. While searching under the sofa for her phone Chloe came across a screwed-up piece of notepaper, she read what was written then burst into tears. While Ruth comforted her, Ben then read the note. *Dear Chloe, I am going to make YOUR wish come true! I am coming with you when you return home! Lots of love, Lucy.*

LYTHAM

It was a warm July morning as the black BMW parked up behind the police car. The two detectives, DI Charles (Chas) Newton and DS Myles Clough walked down the sandy beach of Lytham St Anne's toward the crime scene.

"So, what have we got here Doc?" said Chas as he looked down at the body of a man lying behind a sand dune. "And good morning to you Detective Newton, said Doctor Nigel Evans, pointedly, we have a well-dressed male wearing an expensive 2-piece suit, collar and tie, but no shoes or socks, he is aged 47 and is named Sandy McAvoy."

"So, it's Sandy on the sand with no sandals," said Myles. Silence. "Yes, well, don't you read the local paper? there is a wallet but no mobile and before you ask, he was suffocated."

Chas knelt and touched the body, "He's dry so not been in the sea." Doctor Evans agreed, then added "This is the unusual thing, he has a shredded wheat forced into his mouth."

"Shredded wheat?" asked Myles. "Yes, DS Clough replied Evans, a healthy breakfast cereal provided you don't add sugar," he replied sarcastically." He then moved to the bare feet, "Look here at the soles, a number of cuts, possibly from a stanley-knife, the blood is on the sand, so it was done here." He stood up brushing his hands, "I'll have more details Charles when I've examined him at the Lab, death occurred sometime between 2am to 4am this morning."

"Thank you Nigel, Oh, who found the body?" "The usual" he replied nodding towards a man sitting on a dune, "A dog walker, about 9 am, a PC has taken his statement.

As they walked to the car Chas told Myles to go back to the Station and do a background check on McAvoy and dig out the local paper.

After visiting the widow Chas returned to his office. He called the team together in the incident room to share intelligence. " The victim is Sandy McAvoy owner of The Belmont Gentleman's Club in Blackpool, his wife is Victoria and two children, Trevor and Zac. When I spoke to Victoria earlier today, she told me she wasn't worried when Sandy did not return home on Sunday night as he often stayed at the Club when he worked late. He was well liked and had no enemies, although she does remember hearing a fierce argument he had will his business partner Cecil Lloyd who wanted to expand the business by adding a walk-in restaurant and bar. The Club's finances are fine."

DC Sloan put up his hand, "Yes John." "The house-to-house on the properties across from the beach showed, via a security camera from one of the houses, a grey Ford Focus stopping on the road and a man getting out and walking down the beach, the car drove away. We got the registration." "OK everyone carry on."

Chas and Myles visited The Belmont and spoke to Cecil Lloyd. "We wanted a word with you about Mr McAvoy," asked Chas. "Yes, indeed, such dreadful news, Victoria told me earlier." "We understand you argued with him about the Club," said Myles. "Oh that, nothing of any note." "Quite a heated argument we gather," continued Myles. Lloyd became uncomfortable, "You don't think I murdered him over an argument, do you?" There was a pause, then Chas spoke, "Where were you between 11pm Sunday and 7am Monday morning?"

"Let me think, I was here at the Club with Sandy, I left about 11.30 and went home." Chas continued, "Is there anything else about that night that you remember." Lloyd thought for a moment, "Sandy did get a phone call around 11pm." "Mobile or landline?" "Landline actually, he did seem a bit odd after the call." "How do you mean?" "He was distant, nervous, said he had to go out, he just sat there staring, I felt a bit uneasy so went home."

"Thank you, Mr Lloyd, that'll be all for now." Chas and Myles turned to leave, as they reached the office door Myles looked back, "Do either of you own a grey Ford Focus?" "No Detective."

Back at the Station Chas asked the team for an update. DC Beckett told him the car was a minicab belonging to Ace Cabs, they picked up McAvoy from The Belmont and dropped him off along the beach at Lytham at about midnight. "OK lads, "Oi" and Sarah of course, he added smiling."

That evening Myles and his wife Pauline went to Chas's house for another of June's tasty Spagbol's. "This is no ordinary murder said Chas, it was something more personal, the shredded wheat and the cuts on the feet, was it someone from his past? The cereal suggests something that had happened at breakfast time, perhaps." "But the cuts, where does that fit in," asked Myles. "We need to look into McAvoy's early life and family, Myles." "Can do, Guv, sorry we're off duty, can do, Chas." They both laughed.

Tuesday morning at the Station and the autopsy results were in. The body contained traces of rohypnol. There was bruising on the nose, suggesting it was squeezed tightly shut until suffocation, also severe bruising on the buttocks, tests proved it was caused by driftwood.

Myles looked up as Chas entered the office, "What's new?" Myles showed him the autopsy results, he read the file, "Jeez, this just gets weirder."

"I found the local paper Guv, a story features McAvoy as Businessman of the Year, blah,blah, wife , two adored children, regular donations to good causes and so on." "Good said Chas, did you find anything out about his early life?" Myles told him what he'd found out.

McAvoy grew up in Blackpool with his young brother called Barry. 30 years ago, their parents were killed in a car crash, Barry was in the car but survived.

Social Services allowed the 17-year-old Sandy to bring up 9-year-old Barry in the family home. 12 months later Sandy was off to university so Barry was fostered, long term in Lytham-St-Anne's. "That's all Guv." "Well done mate."

"Have we got the carers details?" "Yep, Mr Mrs Packham, both alive and well – shall we visit?" Chas thought for a moment, "Why not, it's a bit of a long shot, I mean 30 years ago but we must find this Barry he could tell us who had it in for Sandy. Of course, he might be dead." "I know Guv, I can't find out anything about him, it's like he's just dropped off the radar. They arrived at 88 Telford Road and rang the bell. "Good afternoon sir, I'm DI Newton and this is DS Clough, are you Arthur Packham?" "Yes I am, please come in." They talked.

Arthur told them that after 3 years Sandy returned from Uni with his degree in Business studies. Barry wanted to stay with the Packham's, Sandy agreed or was relieved, as Arthur put it, two years later they adopted him, he became Barry Packham. Chas and Myles looked at each other and nodded. Five years later he got a job at the Tower and moved into a bedsit. His visits with the Packham's became less and less – then nothing. Arthur also said he was a quiet boy and didn't talk much, but he was kind and thoughtful. The last time they visited the bedsit he had gone.

"What do we do now Guv ?" said Myles as they sat drinking coffee in a Starbucks café. "Well, we could check with the Tower for a forwarding address, but 20 years ago, not much chance. "No, said Myles I think we should forget about Barry and concentrate on that Lloyds geyser, my money's on him."

Chas stood in the incident room and stared at the evidence board, what is it I've missed he thought. Suddenly DC Steele rushed up to him, "Guv there's something you should see, I looked again at that house-to-house security tape, I ran it for about an hour and look what I found." Chas leaned in, he saw the beach then a dog close to the road, it stopped suddenly turned and ran back toward the sand dunes and out of sight. "Play it back and pause it when the dog gets close." Sarah did, "It looks like a cairn terrier Guv." "It does Sarah, you genius, Myles over here look at this, where have you seen that dog before?" "The McAvoy crime scene, Guv." Chas shouted across the room, "Beckett, fetch the dog walkers' statement in the McAvoy file." He read the name, Brendan Jordan and the address, 52 Dale Street, Blackpool. "Grab your coat Myles, we've got him."

They arrived at the address and knocked on the door, after a while an old lady with a walking stick opened the front door, they showed her their warrant cards, "Does Brendan Jordan live here marm." "No Officer just me, alone." "No problem, sorry to have bothered you." The woman closed the door. "Right Myles, back to the factory."

They sat silently in Chas's office. Then suddenly Chas looked up, "I've got it, the dog." "Not with you Guv." He carried on, where do you take it when it's ill?" "The vet." "Yes, the vet, see how many there are in the Blackpool area." A few clicks on his phone, 18, Guv."

They went into the main office, "Listen up everyone, Chas shouted, there are 18 vets in the area I want to split them up between us and phone asking if they had ever treated a white cairn terrier, if yes, get the name and address, let's do it.

One hour late a result, DC Breach gave Chas the details, Balmoral Road Lytham-St-Annes. A white cairn terrier treated for a small chicken bone stuck in the throat. Owner Barry Packham, 71 Marsden Street, Lytham.

The tall thin bearded man sat in the interview room alone. Chas and Myles entered and sat down; Chas did all the talking. The man confirmed his name was Barry Packman aged 38. He was asked if he wanted a solicitor present, he said no. The tape was switched on and the interview began.

"OK Barry we're here to talk about the death of your brother Sandy, but first, why did you give a false name and address to the policeman at the crime scene?" "Because I thought you would blame ME." "Fair enough, now would you tell us about your childhood?"

Barry said yes and began, "I had a very happy childhood until the car crash, did you know about that?" "Yes, we do."He continued. " Sandy asked me what happened in the car I told him I was playing my mouth organ Dad told me to stop he turned to look at me then Mum screamed Dad turned back the traffic had stopped moving we crashed into a big lorry. Sandy became very angry, said the crash was my fault. From that day on he was horrible to me. I dreaded it when he said it was bath-time, when I finished washing, he would pull me forward over the edge of the bath and beat me on the bottom with a stick, when he finished he'd walk out of the bathroom saying 'Get dressed'. Barry looked at Chas, "Shall I go on?" "Please do."

"At breakfast he asked what cereal I liked, I said cornflakes he said tough you're having shredded wheat or nothing. One morning over breakfast I was drinking my milk when he leaned across the table and smacked my head saying drink quietly, the shock made me drop the glass which shattered on the floor, he came round the table and made me stand on the broken glass then shouted 'jump up and down', the pain was awful, 'now clean it up and go to school' he shouted. I sat on the floor and watched as the milk and blood mixed together."

By now Barry was sobbing quietly. Chas's mobile rang, "I must take this he said to Myles, back in a minute." Now Barry, can you remember where you were last Monday morning between 1am and 7am," asked Myles. "I work nights as a security guard at the Morton Retail Park, I was there from 9pm Sunday until 5am Monday. " "Can anyone confirm that?" "Yes, there were three of us on duty there."

Chas re-entered the room, " We'll take a break now, I'm sure you'd like a coffee and perhaps something to eat." Chas then called for a uniformed WPC who took Barry to the canteen. "What's going on Guv?" "We need to talk Myles." They went to Chas's office.

"That phone call was from Cecil Lloyd, said Chas, he wants to change his statement, the call on Sunday night was from Victoria, Sandy's wife, she must have a connection with Barry, so I phoned Beckett and told him to go to the Lytham vet with a photo of Victoria, I'm just waiting now for his call. His mobile rang, it was Beckett.

The receptionist remembered seeing Victoria, she had brought her dog in for a minor complaint. She also noticed that she and Barry were deep in conversation.

"Thanks Beckett, good work," said Chas. Myles then told him Barry's alibi. "Shall I bring her in Guv?" "Yes, and organise a search of the house." "What about a Warrant?" Chas smiled, "I don't think Lloyd will object, I'll release Barry."

Victoria sat next to her solicitor, opposite sat Chas and Myles. The tape was switched on.

"Where were you Mrs McAvoy, asked Chas, between 11pm last Sunday night and 7am Monday morning." "At home, Detective." "Did you make any phone calls during that time?" "No, I was in bed asleep." Chas looked down at the file then looked up, "We have a witness who said you phoned your husband at 11pm." "Ah, yes, I remember now, I asked him when he would be home as it was getting late." Chas again looked at the file, "But when I spoke to you on Monday you said Sandy often slept at the Club when he worked late which didn't worry you." "Do you know a man called Barry Packham? "No." "We have a witness who says you do, you like lying don't you Mrs McAvoy?" "All right, all right she shouted, I can't take any more of this," and burst into tears."

When calm she told Chas and Myles the truth. She started by talking about Sandy, "Everyone thought he was this great family man, his donations to charities, they made him Businessman of The Year for God's sake. The truth is he beat me if I spoke out of turn or disagreed with him. Then there was his womanising, he thought I didn't know."

Myles slid a box of tissues across the table. "The last straw was when I found out his latest girlfriend was only 15 years old.

"Tell us about Barry," asked Chas. " Well, when my dog became ill I took her to the vet, in the waiting-room he and I struct up a conversation, we just clicked, it's true what they say about being able to unload your problems with a stranger. It was when Barry said his bullying brother had been made Businessman of the year, I decided what to do."

She phoned Sandy told something terrible has happened and they had to talk, she then told him where to meet. She arrived before him armed with the rohypnol, a bottle of whisky, a Stanley knife, and the shredded wheat. A piece of driftwood lay nearby.

"Well, you know what happened next, I don't regret what I did." Chas stroked his chin, So, because of your actions you knew Barry would be arrested for murder, how could you do that, knowing how he'd suffered as a child." "It had to be done, I'm sorry about Barry, but that man had to die."

She was formally charged with murder and remanded in custody. There was one more thing Chas wanted to do.

The doorbell of 88 Telford Road chimed, Arthur Packham opened the door, "Hello Detective, what can I do for you?" "I've brought someone to see you." He moved and Barry stepped forward, "Hello Dad." Arthur, with tears in his eyes, hugged him tightly.

Chas silently left the scene; he wiped a tear from his eye as he headed for his car.

ROBIN'S QUEST

Not far from Farnham is Lonsdale Village. There are a few shops a Village Hall, a Church, and Lonsdale Infants School.

Victor Jellicoe, the school caretaker, was a jolly, chubby, red-faced man who hailed from Bristol. He had a wife, Moira and a five-year-old son called Robin who attended the school.

There was great excitement one morning as the whole school had gathered on the lawned area beside a hole Victor had dug earlier. The previous week the Headmistress and staff had announced they were going bury a time-capsule. The children had helped decide what was to go in it. So, at 10am the capsule, which was a steel box, was lowered into the ground amid great cheering and clapping. When everyone had gone back indoors, Victor filled in the hole and placed an inscribed brass plaque on top to mark the spot.

A few days later, one playtime, Robin, and his best friend Susan Page, both aged 6, decided to bury their own capsule next to an oak tree. Susan had brought from home an old, unwanted, metal cashbox. The two children put various things into it then dug a hole using trowels borrowed from the class garden box then buried it.

One morning at 11.30 Victor was in the hall laying out the tables and benches for lunch at noon. Two children crossed the hall on their way to the library. "Hello Mr. Jelly" they called out. "Hello m'dears" he answered. Now they called him Mr. Jelly not only because of his name but, as one child put it 'He has a wobbly tummy'. It was always said with affection. The children all love Victor. Nothing was ever too much; he would repair broken possessions or sometimes do magic tricks. One time during 'book week' he nailed blocks of wood to a pair of shoes and dressed in waistcoat and baggy trousers and spent the day in school as the BFG (big friendly giant).

Unfortunately, his aim for authenticity went a bit too far. It was decided one morning to have a fire drill. When the alarm sounded all teachers and children moved slowly and quietly into the playground. To make things more realistic Victor got hold of a disco smoke machine. He aimed it towards an open classroom door. When the children saw the smoke pouring out, they started wailing and crying, thinking their school was burning down. Mrs Morgan, the headmistress, spotted Victor she waved jazz-hands at him to stop. Which he did. He never lived it down. It caused much merriment in the staffroom.

Anyway, life went on. When the children outgrew Lonsdale Infants. They went to St. Mary's Junior school. After this it was on to Farnham Comprehensive. But, alas, Robin went there alone. Susan and family had emigrated to Australia.

Robin eventually went to university. While there he met and fell in love with Maria Willcox. They both loved building design and construction so were aiming for a BA(Hons.) Architecture. After graduating, both got jobs with different design firms in London. Love blossomed and they were married two years later and bought a house in West London.

Their honeymoon in Italy did not go quite so smoothly. They stayed at the Marco Polo Hotel in Campalto. Midweek a boat ride took the honeymooners to Venice. As they approached the dock the beauty of the Doges Palace greeted them. The day went very well until as they walked along a narrow street towards St. Mark's Square and the Basilica, Maria, wearing flipflops, tripped and fell heavily to the ground. A man brought a chair from a nearby shop, some people picked Maria up and placed her gently on the chair. Blood was running from her knee.

Robin was overwhelmed by the noise and the people. Medics arrived and took her away. Robin had no idea where Maria had been taken to. He roamed the streets, the squares, and crossed bridges, asking where the hospital was, but no joy until he met an English couple who gave him directions. On reaching the hospital he rushed up to the reception window. "My wife, Maria Jellicoe" was all he could say. The woman looked at her computer screen. "Dimesso Dall'ospedale", she said. A man who was stood nearby said "Discharged, she's been discharged". Robin sat down on a waiting room chair with his head in his hands. Where is she now, he thought. He was pleased though that she wasn't seriously hurt. Suddenly he had an idea. Leaving the hospital, he made his way back to St. Mark's Square, then running down the Piazza San Marco towards the sea he then turned left and headed toward the boat they had arrived in. There she stood. He ran towards her and she to him. It was like a scene from a romantic French movie. "Oh, darling Maria I was so worried I'd never find you again. "I'm fine my love, just fine" she said as tears rolled down her cheeks. "What about your knee?" "It was just a cut. No stitches, just bandaged, I'm good". The rest of the holiday went without a hitch.

About 5 weeks after the honeymoon Robin received an invitation to attend an Architectural Conference in Melbourne, Australia. It would be in a months' time. Maria agreed he should go, so he accepted.

Thinking about Australia reminded him of his friend Susan Page. He hadn't seen her for 20 years I wonder if she is still living there.

Robin remembered her parent's names were Steven and Gina. He opened his computer and started scrolling through various sites. He found them. They lived in a cul-de-sac called Dorset Close, in Croydon, a suburb of Melbourne. As he read on, news of a shocking tragedy unfolded. He couldn't believe it. The Page family had previously lived in a detached house that had caught fire. Apparently one evening Steven and Gina had gone to the theatre, Susan remained at home, she had taken a sleeping pill and gone to bed. It was not known, conclusively, how the fire started. The house burnt down, and Susan died.

The Inkerman Conference Centre was only about 30 miles from Dorset Close. Robin managed to get hold of the Page's phone number and gave them a call.

He could hear the sadness in Steven's voice as he spoke to him. Robin asked if he could visit them. Yes, he would be very welcome he was told, anyone from Susan's past would be a blessing.

Robin's flight was in 3 weeks' time. The first thing he did after speaking to Steven was visit his dad Victor who was still the caretaker at Lonsdale Infants School. Together they went to the big oak tree near the playground. They dug up the cashbox, then returned to the bungalow. After a long chat with his mum and dad, Robin hugged them and returned home.

As he walked down Dorset Close, Robin was feeling very nervous, I mean, 20 years, he thought. He knocked on the door and stood back. The door opened and both Steven and Gina were there to greet him. They couldn't have made it any plainer that they were pleased to see him. Over tea and cake the three of them chatted. Then the dreadful truth came out. Gina, clutching a handkerchief, told Robin how everything they owned had perished. And worst of all nothing of Susan had survived, no photo's, letters or belongings, nothing.

It was then Robin placed the carrier bag he had brought with him, on to the coffee table. He gently removed the cashbox and put it down in front of them. "Open it", he said. With shaking hands, Steven opened the box, he put his hand to his mouth and gasped. He removed the items that Susan had placed there all those years ago; a woollen bracelet she had made, a plastic ring, a red balloon, and a mars bar wrapper. They chuckled. "She loved Mars Bars", said Gina. At the bottom of the box was an envelope that Robin had put there. "Now what's this" said Steven as he opened it. They both burst into tears and hugged each other when they saw a photo of Susan in her school uniform. First Steven kissed the picture then Gina. Looking in the envelope Gina withdrew a letter written by Susan. In her spidery writing, she wrote: *Hello, my name is Susan Page. My mummy is called gina and my daddy is called steven. I love them very very much they are the best in the world. My best frend is robin. I hope you like what I have put in here, goodbye.*

Susan's parents were overcome. "We can't thank you enough Robin, we now have something of Susan's to treasure," said Steven. Robin swallowed hard. "There's something else". He withdrew an 8x10 photograph from the bag and placed it face down on the table. "I spoke to my dad, and this is the result". He turned the photo over. It was a picture of the school library, on one wall was a sign which read, The Susan Page Library, underneath was a picture of Susan in her school uniform. "Just something for others to remember her by".

⸺◄❖►⸺

THE HOMESTEAD

It was the 1ˢᵗ of January 2000 as the staff of Gracedale Manor rose early to tidy up after the millennium party the previous evening. The Butler, Jasper Jenkins visited each room to ensure everything was 'tip top'. He then visited the kitchen to check on breakfast for Robert Wrensdale, Earl of Gracedale and guests. His wife Mary was the head cook. "Calm down Jasper, everything will be fine". He sat down. "Darling it was SOME Party last night, but you're right, I'll calm down, any coffee going?".

Breakfast was served at 9am instead of the usual 8am. It was a very quiet affair as the guests discussed what life would be like in this 21ˢᵗ Century. Later that morning Lord Wrensdale took Jasper aside. "Well done for last night and this morning". "Thank you, sir,". Wrensdale then lowered his voice and tapped the side of his nose. "You will be visiting 'Homestead' I expect, to check internet connection, especially after all that talk in the press about signal failure". Yes sir, I'm on my way".

Things were not quite what they seem. Jasper's real name was Rex Williams. He was born in 1957 and qualified as a Civil Engineer in the late 1970's. After completing a military career as a Major in the SAS and together with his engineering experience, he was offered a post with MI6. He accepted. He led a secret mission code named 'The Homestead'. His task was to design a state-of-the-art Bunker. The difference being above ground instead of below. There will, of course, be an extensive basement. The idea was a building hiding in plain sight.

The 4-bedroom house was built in the grounds of Gracedale Manor with the permission of Lord Wrensdale (also with MI6). Rex, then undercover as Jenkins the Butler, lived with his wife in the house. He could come and go without suspicion and still be able to update and modify the property.

Now, in 2022, Rex 'retired' as Butler yet was allowed to live in the house as a gift from Wrensdale for his loyal service. All quite acceptable to the outside world. By now Mary had died so Rex continued his work alone. Apart from his MI6 Handler.

Sean Black was a very nasty 28-year-old. He was married to Alex, and they had a 4-year-old daughter called Gemma. Both had suffered physical abuse. Black had spent 2 years in Borstal and 3 years in prison for theft and violence. A man with a very short temper. He could be charming when he chose to like when he was courting Alex. She, unfortunately, witnessed his 'other' side, AFTER they were married. He worked as a night-club Doorman at weekends and thieving during the week. He noticed the House once while driving past the Manor Estate. Several visits later, he noticed the house was some distance from the Manor, good he thought. Using binoculars, he established what appeared to be just one old man with a walking stick living there. Sometimes a woman would visit but not very often. Taking this place will be easy, he thought.

One Tuesday in October, around 6pm, Rex was in the basement checking food stocks when the silent alarm tripped. A red light in the ceiling flashed. Going immediately to the basement office he checked the CCTV screens. He saw a tall man enter the sitting-room. Rex climbed the basement stairs then turned and entered a concealed study. He triggered, by remote, the sitting-room door. It swiftly shut and locked. He then slid open a false wall in the study and stepped into the room.

The man had his back to him as he fiddled with the door handle. Rex moved forward very slowly as he reached for his walking stick and raised it slightly as he pressed a button on the side. Immediately a 4-inch needle appeared at the end of the stick. He approached the man and plunged the needle into his leg. The man screamed, turned, then fell unconscious to the floor. Using his mobile phone, Rex took a picture of the man's face. He then called Lizzie Mays, his MI6 Handler. "Hi Rex, what's the problem?" "Hi Liz, a male intruder, tall, late twenties. Nothing above 'Level 3', just a thief, I think. I'll send his photo. Tell you more later, bye Liz". "Understood, bye Rex".

He dragged the man into the study and sat him on a steel chair beside his desk. Sitting down on the other side Rex pressed a button under the desktop, the man's chair became bolted to the floor, another button caused the steel manacles on the arms of the chair to snap shut over his wrists.

Rex poured himself a scotch and stared at the stranger who had started to come round. "What's going on, why am I stuck in this chair?" Rex replied, "Don't speak, all will be explained". "This gaff ain't up to much, I got through the front door easy". "You were meant to. Rather than failing to get in then going away, we want to find out who you are. You see, you're the fly and I'm the spider, now shut up". The phone rang, it was Lizzie. Rex answered, as he listened, he jotted down notes on a pad. "I got all that Liz, oh, would you send over a couple of lads for backup?". "Will do, bye".

Rex looked up from his notes, "Firstly, what's your name?" "What's yours, twat". "OK stranger, question 2, how much pain can you take?" The stranger sat bolt upright. "Sean Black, that's my name". "Good, how long have you known Ivan Isovich? "I don't know any Igor Sonofabitch". No, the name is Ivan Is-o-vitch, how long?"

Sean started squirming in the chair, "Look, bastard, you can't keep me here like this, call the police or let me go". Rex smiled, "The word around here is 'No police, no release'." Rex noticed the cctv screen on his desk. Two men were standing outside the front door dressed as tradesmen. Using the intercom phone, he asked "Where are you?" One of the men replied, "Outside the Homestead". The front door opened, and the two men entered and made for the study, then stood either side of the prisoner. "Our friend here doesn't feel like talking, lock him in the cell". Rex then released the manacles. The two agents handcuffed Sean and took him down to the basement.

Sean Black's wife, Alex, after two days, began to worry where her husband was. No, not worry, hoped he wasn't coming back. She allowed herself to smile, to go to bed at night without fear. Her daughter Gemma began to blossom, to talk more. Alex invited some friends over. She thought it wouldn't last.

On day 4, Rex had a meeting with Lizzie. They discussed the prisoner's testimony that claimed Isovich handed him money outside the nightclub (recorded on cctv) as payment for supplying a 'willing girl' as he put it. He did not pass secrets or agree to work for him. They both decided, after investigation, Isovich was a low-key suspect. Things would go no further. "What'll I do with matey?" asked Rex. Lizzie paused for a moment, "Show him 'Warcroft'. They shook hands and she left the house.

On day 5 the prisoner was brought to Rex's study and secured in the chair. "Right is there anything you want to add to your previous statements?" asked Rex. "Yea, he leaned forward, go shoot yourself". Rex smiled "How apposite, you shot an associate of Isovich, what was his name?"

Sean's eyes looked left and right; he shifted uneasily in the chair. "Dunno what you're talking about". Rex leaned back and cupped his hands behind his head. "No matter, we're not concerned with a basic murder here, that's one for the police". He leaned forward, hands on the desk. "But, when we discovered you were dabbling in drug dealing with foreign terrorists, that's a whole new ball-game". "Am I leaving here or not?" Rex looked down at his laptop, tapped a few keys then swung the screen around to face Sean, "Watch this chap", he said. The screen showed a young man wearing a grey suit, his face was covered with an animal mask. He began ranting about two African countries. His diatribe apart from being racist was a demand for both African Presidents to be jailed for violence. (Totally untrue). After 10 minutes the picture went blank. Sean looked up. "So, what's that gotta do with me?" Rex smiled. "Well old chap, that is you". "You're crazy, man, that 'aint me". Rex swung the laptop back round and closed it saying, "No it's a mockup, could be you, the mask helps. You see, you have now become an asset". Sean stared blankly. Rex continued. "We have been showing that little rant online for the past 3 days". "So what?" "Well, old bean, when we told the Africans, through 'Intelligence' we know who the racist is, the reply was, sent him to us, we'll owe you. So, there you have it. Rex paused for a moment then continued. Help from Africa will come in very handy in the future". Sean started wriggling and shouting. "You can't do that to me, you can't". ignoring him, Rex produced a file, "Read what it says, there on the cover above the words 'Top Secret' ". No reply. "It says Warcroft". Still no reply. "It's your real name, Warren Croft. We know just about everything about you". Rex picked up the desk phone and said one word, "Now." He then turned to Warren saying, "Don't worry about your wife and daughter, they will be rehoused and financially secure.

The two agents entered the room, Rex stood and picked up his walking stick. "Did you know, Warren, this has a biblical reference?" He pushed the needle into the now crying man's stomach, I call it my Kane and disable stick." Warren didn't hear him.

⫸⫷

GREENWAYS

A beautiful 4-bedroom detached house nestled in the surrey countryside was bought in 1940 by Mr and Mrs Danvers. Harry and Daisy were newly married and went on to have 3 children, The twins John and Jason and their younger sister Jennifer. All looked lovely from the outside but inside, not so much. The children had a very sad childhood, it's true they wanted for nothing, well fed, and well-dressed but what they wanted most of all was love. Their parents were always out and about, enjoying themselves, theatre, dinner parties or drinking. The closest the children came to a parent was Nanny Roberts, but she wasn't always there. From the age of 10 the boys were left to look after their 7-year-old sister at night-time. Over time they felt alone, isolated. They formed a 3-way bond, always looking out for each other. One time in junior school, Jennifer was being bullied by an older boy. The twins stepped in, John punched the bully and Jason warned him "Never touch her again". That was all that was said. Two boys of few words.

Later that day, sitting in their classroom the teacher called them to come forward. He stood with a bamboo cane in his right hand. He looked at them for a moment. "One of you assaulted a boy earlier today". John spoke up, "he was hurting our sister". "Never mind that which one of you hurt the boy?" Silence, they just stared at the teacher. "Come on now, which one?" Silence. "OK then I will have to cane you both". Instantly, John gripped the teacher's right wrist tightly, Jason gripped the left, saying, "if you cane both of us, knowing one of us is innocent, that is child abuse". John continued, "We shall call the Police". They released their grip but continued to stare at the teacher. Visibly shaken, he backed down. "Very well then let this be a warning to you, now sit down". As the twins sat down, they turned to look at each other and smiled.

On another occasion some years later the sibling's motto 'Justice not Injustice' continued. When Jennifer was 17, she was walking home from college when she heard someone following her, when she stopped, they stopped when she continued, they continued, she phoned the boys.

As they approached Jennifer, they saw a man standing over her. Jason circled round behind him. John shouted "Oi". The man looked up then turned to run but instead felt a fist hit him full in the face. He went down. Between them, they broke both his legs. The three then walked home in silence. 'Oi' was the only word spoked throughout the episode.

When their parents died, Greenways became theirs. The 3-way bond continued. They never married or had children. They set up a dry cleaning and laundry business that became very successful. John managed the firm's books. Everything would have jogged along nicely except for one thing. John was a gambler; poker was his addiction and he lost – big time. He had started to drain money from the business. In July 1995 things came to a head, when losing badly during a game he gambled Greenways to win – he lost. The winner, a notorious figure, gave John 2 weeks to empty the house and move out.

Jennifer and Jason were inconsolable especially when they found out how badly the business had suffered. The deeds to the house were handed over to the new owner a Maurice Cole.

They sold everything they could including two of their three cars. The dry-cleaning shop was sold but they kept the launderette as a source of income. They remained together albeit in a dingy rented flat.

Part 2.

It was summer 2005 when the car turned into Vallance Close then into the drive of number 10 called Greenways. The Mason family had arrived at their new home.

The first to enter the house was Charles Mason, a doctor, his wife Violet an artist, then their two children Gary aged 10 and Nancy aged 6. After the removal lorry had left the family had a bit of a sort out then had an early night.

It was the first week of August. After the move Charles started work at the Eastside Hospital while Violet stayed at home where she designed greeting cards and sold them online. The children were of course on school holidays. One morning there was a knock at the door, Violet answered and saw an old couple on the doorstep. "Good morning said the man, my name is Reginald Bolt, and this is my wife Frances, we live next door at number 8". Violet smiled, "so pleased to meet you, I'm Violet Mason", Reginald proffered the cake he was holding, "just a little housewarming gift, Frances made it". Violet invited them in for coffee, they accepted. The children looked up from the board game they were playing as their mum introduced them. After a lovely chat, coffee and cake, the Bolts bid farewell. "What do you think of our neighbours?" Violet asked the children. "He was a sailor," said Gary. "Yes, and she was a sailoress" added Nancy. Violet laughed, "both in the navy, what about that, anyway, let's get lunch ready".

A few days later the Bolts came over for dinner after the children were in bed. Violet told them how she planned to landscape the garden as it looked 'pretty drab' as she put it. The Bolts thought that was a great idea, then asked where they had lived before coming to the close. "We lived in a little village in Yorkshire said Charles, then the strangest thing happened, you see this house used to belong to my mum and dad" "What was his name asked Frances?" "Oh, Maurice Cole". "But I thought your name was Mason". "Well actually Frances, my full name is Charles Cole-Mason, I was adopted but I wanted to keep my birth name, but it's all a bit of a mouthful, anyway, one day they both upped and left, they were never seen again, we of course were living in Yorkshire. My guess is they decided to live in a more exotic country, he was in the import-export business". Charles paused for a moment. "Still, it's odd they never got in touch with me. Well, the house remained empty for several years and as there was no word from Maurice it was made over to me being his only living relative. Of course, I was obliged to rescind ownership if he returned.

Over the following weeks the Bolts often visited the Masons. The couple who lived at number 12 pretty much kept themselves to themselves.

Arriving home one afternoon after collecting Gary and Nancy from school the children ran into the kitchen to get a snack, "WOW", said Gary loudly. Violet, intrigued, joined them. All the kitchen wall-unit doors were stood wide open. "Did you do that mummy?" asked Nancy. "No, I did not", she replied as she closed the doors. "We must have a ghost then", suggested Gary. "Don't be silly love, come on now get a snack then do your homework. The incident did bother her though. After telling Charles about it later that evening, he thought it was probably a gust of wind on opening the front door, "It's an old house darling, don't worry about it".

It happened again two days later, except this time the chairs around the dining table were lying flat on the floor. Well, that wasn't the wind, thought Violet. A week later things turned more sinister. The children's games-cupboard door was open and a pack of playing cards were strewn over the dining room table. Charles and Violet discussed this latest 'happening' and reluctantly agreed it may be some sort of haunting. They decided to ask the Bolts about the history of the house.

On the Saturday morning around 11am they were stood by the front door of number 8. As Violet reached forward to press the bell the sound of an ambulance as it entered Vallance Close could be heard. They both looked round as it backed into number 8. Suddenly the front door opened and Frances, eyes red and clutching a hanky stepped out, she was startled to see them then blurted out "My Reginald has had a heart attack". The Masons were shocked to see this normally happy smiling woman now looking so sad and distraught.

They returned home and told the children the sad news. Later, Charles spoke to Violet. "I'm on morning shift tomorrow so I'll ask how he's doing". On the Sunday afternoon when Charles returned home, he told Violet that Reginald was comfortable and would be kept in for observation. To cheer everyone up he rounded up the children "Shall we go out for dinner?" "Yea" was the reply. "OK kids your choice". They ended up at McDonalds. The children's choice!

They left the restaurant and returned home, as they pulled into the drive Nancy shouted excitedly "Look Mr Bolt is waving at us". Charles and Violet looked at each other, then at the lounge window, sure enough there he was, waving. Slowly they got out of the car telling the children to walk behind him and mummy. On reaching the front door and entering they went into the lounge, no one there. After looking everywhere and calling his name there was no sign of him. Violet told Gary and Nancy it was just a trick of the light. After the children were in bed Charles poured two glasses of merlot and joined Violet on the sofa. "Well, my love, tell me, are you thinking what I'm thinking?", she asked. Charles looked at her, "You mean this is some sort of omen of death?" "Yes, I do, I don't want to go all 'paranormal activity' on you but if this IS a haunted house, perhaps we should move, things might get worse". Charles sipped his wine, "look darling, when I'm at Eastside tomorrow I'll check up on Reginald and perhaps you could call and speak to the Stevens at number 12. Ask them about the history of our house".

What a lovely looking house thought Violet, she was impressed by the perfectly manicured front lawn and flower beds. She sounded the large shiny brass knocker on the dark green front door. Mrs Stevens answered, "Mrs Mason, isn't it?" she asked. "Oh, Violet, please, I just wondered if we could have a little chat, if you're not too busy?" She was invited inside and over tea and biscuits they discussed 'Greenways'.

When Charles returned home the look on his face told Violet the news was not good. He hugged her, "I'm afraid love, Reginald has died". Later Violet told him about her visit to number 12. She was told about the poker game for the house, 'common knowledge' as Mrs Stevens put it. How the Danvers, John, Jason, and Jennifer had to move out. They were never heard of again. She asked Violet if they had ever heard from Maurice. On hearing the news about how his father had won the house playing poker shocked Charles, that poor family that had to move out, he thought, it must have been awful for them.

The next day Violet picked the children up from school as usual, when they were all in the car heading home Gary suddenly said, "I saw Mr Bolt today", "so did I ", added Nancy. Violet pulled over and stopped the car. It seems he was in the car park as they came out of school. She was cross that they hadn't said something before getting in the car. When they arrived home Violet went into the kitchen, it was there she saw it.

As Charles came through the front door Violet rushed forward, "We need to talk". They went into the kitchen and closed the door. She then showed him the note that was taped to the fridge door, it read, 'Move house soon there is danger ahead', the writing was bright red done with a felt tip pen to look like blood. She then told him what the children had said. "Oh my God, this is bad we'll talk later", he replied. When they were alone Charles said again, "This is bad, I'd say this note is a threat, wouldn't you?" Violet agreed. He continued; "I think Bolt wanted us out, God rest his soul, all this haunting is just a ruse and now this note". But

Violet wasn't convinced, "how do you explain Reginald being dead then appearing again and how does he keep getting into the house?" "I don't know, darling, Let's just tell the police everything and see want they think, agreed?" "Agreed".

Part 3.

Charles and Violet arrived at Eastside Police Station and asked to speak to someone in CID. Detective Sergeant Sam Waite came down to Reception and asked them to follow him. They entered Interview Room 2 sat down and told him their story. "So, you don't believe the whole haunting thing?" "We did at first, said Charles, but not after we got this note", he slid it across the table. Sam studied the message, "I suppose it could be considered a threat, but that does not explain this Reginald chap dying then appearing again to your whole family". Violet chipped in "Perhaps it's a Reginald lookalike". "That's possible, but why would the Bolts want you to move house?" "My theory is, said Charles, the Bolts were forced out and now want it back". DI Waite stood up, "well that's a possible explanation, leave it with me, I'll look into it and get back to you". Charles and Violet then stood, shook hands with Sam, thanked him and then left the police station. On their way home they agreed he took them seriously and didn't laugh at them.

At 8 Vallance Close Frances was still heartbroken over the death of Reginald. She was sitting in the lounge; two cups of tea were on the coffee table in front of her. She looked up as the lounge door opened. "Hello Ronald, the teas are cold I'm afraid". He crossed the room and sat down opposite her. "We should talk Frances". She looked at him, "the haunting thing didn't work, did it?"

"No, it didn't, he snapped, so we'll have to up our game". Frances looked at him angrily, "what, you mean kill the Masons like you did Cole and his wife and bury them in the back garden of Greenways?" Ronald glared at her, "keep your voice down woman, just let me think what our next move should be". He put his head in his hands for a moment then looked up, "I want that house back".

Charles and Violet had finished lunch and were discussing what might happen next when there was a knock at the door, Violet went to open it and, on the doorstep, stood Frances. "Oh, do come in, I'm so sorry about Reginald". She gave Frances a hug, she was about to close the door when she saw a man standing there, "do come in, you must be a friend of Frances's". Charles joined them and they all went into the lounge. "Please, sit down, he said, then looking at the stranger, asked, I'm sorry I don't know your name". "My name is John Danvers, a friend of Frances's". Charles and Violet exchanged shocked glances. "Well, said Charles, you're Reginald's lookalike". Before the man could answer there was a knock on the lounge door. Everyone turned to look. Violet, looking a bit bewildered, stood up, "Mrs Stevens, err, hello". "No, my name is Jennifer Travers, and this, pointing to a man behind her, is Jason Travers, my brother, now sit down, bitch, and shut up".

Charles and Violet sat transfixed as all the facts were explained to them. John lived at no.8 with Mr and Mrs Bolt, he acted as Mr Bolt, Reginald was never seen. Jason and Jennifer lived at no.12 under the name of Stevens. When asked if they had any questions Violet wanted to know why the Bolts were helping them. Frances told them she and Reginald were also victims of Maurice Cole. Another question was, how did John and Jasper get in the house. John explained, when they came over for dinner, he excused himself to use the cloakroom, found the keys on the hall table and used putty to make a copy. Charles spoke, "so what happens now, I know you want Greenways, if you kill us what happens to our children?"

Jason roared with laughter, "they'll probably be adopted, you know what that's like". John stepped in, "we will buy the house from you at half market value of course, for all the suffering we've been through because of your dad". "We'll give you a week to think it over" added Jennifer. As they all stood up to leave there was a rap at the front door. Charles rushed to answer, in walked DI Waite and two uniformed police officers.

THE EPILOGUE

After the suspects were taken away for questioning, Sam sat down with Charles and Violet to explain things from his end.

He read the file on Greenways. He noticed John and Jason were twins, that would explain the haunting. He searched further back and found all three had, at one time or another, been arrested for violence but never charged, insufficient evidence. Then the mysterious disappearance of Maurice and Rita Cole, the case was unsolved. He then found that in the last two years, bank and financial records showed a steep rise in income. How, unknown. From what they HAD found out about the Danvers they were able to get a search warrant for both no.8 and no.12. As Sam was leaving, he assured them everything would be fine, but then added, "Would you do one thing for me?"

Charles and Violet decided to have family holiday. Together with the children they left home for a week of relaxation and fun. As they drove out of Vallance Close and headed for the main road a police search and forensic team were backing into Greenways to dig up the back garden.

SCHOOLDAYS

George Armstrong aged 13 sat quietly beside his father as they drove through the gates of St Anselm's School and parked the car. This was his first day at the school. The date was 7th September 1975. The family had recently moved from Manchester to Leeds. George loved his old school, his friends and the teachers. "Come on George out you get." We're late Dad, please come in with me," he begged. "Don't be silly, off you go or I'll be late for work." George pleaded with his father but to of no avail. "Look, said his father, as he pointed through the windscreen, there's a woman standing by the front door, go speak to her, hurry now." Reluctantly George got out of the car, closed the door and stood waving as his father drove away. He then turned and walked towards the woman.

25 YEARS LATER

George Armstrong drove his Mercedes slowly through the gates of St Anselm's School, parked the car and entered the building. There was a large reception area with a staircase to the left and the school office to the right. he knocked and entered. A middle-aged woman was sat behind her desk and looked up as he entered. "Good morning, I'm Joyce Dean, School Secretary, can I help you?" She stood up and extended her hand. "Yes indeed, replied George as he shook her hand, I'm from Armstrong Publishing, I have your Stationary Order." That's odd thought Joyce, a delivery man wearing an expensive suit, she glanced out of the window to see his van. "Gosh, do all the delivery men get a Mercedes, you must have a nice Boss?" George smiled, "no they don't and I AM the Boss, George Armstrong at your service." She smiled back. "Really, why the personal visit?" "Well, to be honest I didn't realise we supplied this school and when I saw the address on the order, I wanted to deliver it myself, this is my old school."

"Fancy that, replied Joyce, I'm sure Mr Tate the Headmaster would like to see you, it's not often we have a visit from an 'old boy', have you time to meet him?" "Yes indeed," answered George. He went back to his car collected the order and headed back towards the building, he stopped at the front door, his thoughts went back to his time there, fear and sadness gripped him. As he placed the carton in the office, he asked Joyce if he could have a wander round before meeting the head?" She looked at her watch, "Certainly, Assembly won't be over for another 30 minutes, how about a coffee first?" He nodded. "They called me the 'Ghost' when I was here because I was so good so quiet so shy." George then sat down on a nearby chair. I recall Mr Reid once telling me to stand up during English Lit., Prompt me as to your name boy, I am aware of you and at the say time NOT aware of you, a true enigma, as Glanville put it, some presences haunt and discourage us. Sit down boy. George paused, looked down then looked at Joyce, "He still didn't know my name, anyway, he was quite wrong about Glanville, he said Daunt not haunt, I wonder whether his mistake was genuine of not." The room was silent for a moment. "I'm so sorry Joyce I seem to have got carried away." She looked at him with a sort of sadness in her eyes. "When did you leave here George, I might have some photos you could see?" " I left in 1978." She looked along the bookcase and took down a ring binder. He leafed through it then stopped when he saw a photo of Mr Ross, Joyce looked over his shoulder, "Mr Ross, he's still here, still teaching History, same classroom in fact." George felt sick. "Thank you for your time, Joyce and the coffee, I think I'll go for that wander now." "OK George, see you later." He left the office and made his way up the staircase. On reaching his old classroom he stood outside the door then with a shaking hand turned the knob and entered.

As he stood there the fear returned. He looked around, chairs and desks, newer, but still in the same place, he walked up to the blackboard and slowly paced both palms on the surface then removed them, his sweaty palm-prints showed up clearly on the blackboard. He then turned and walked to the back of the room selected a chair and sat down in the same place he used to sit all those years ago. With his elbows on the desk, he covered his face with his hands. Suddenly, he heard movement, looking up he had gone back in time, the room was full of boys, to his right was Jamie Burton, his best friend.

The teacher, Mr Ross, is writing a heading on the blackboard it says *The Corn Importation Bill.* He speaks, "Johnson, the date please." The boy replies, 25th June 1846, SIR."

"Correct, how then did this affect the Duty, Haslett?"

"Er, reduced the Duty from 18 shillings to 4, SIR."

"Per what Haslett, per what?"

"Per quarter, SIR."

"Bolton, when was the duty reduced to 1 shilling per quarter?"

"After January 1849, SIR."

"Correct. Now boys I want to talk about last Monday's homework. I asked you to name 10 members of the Russell Administration."

It was at this point that Jamie produced a joke spider, when George saw it he screamed in surprise. Mr Ross's ferret like eyes surveyed the class. "Stand up that boy." Nobody moved, he repeated it, only louder this time, slowly George rose to his feet. Mr Ross looked at him with disgust. "Your name boy?" "Armstrong, Sir." "Louder, boy."

"ARMSTRONG, SIR."

"You wanted to say something about the homework?"

"NO, SIR."

"But you interrupted me while I was talking, Armstrong."

"Was that a question, Sir?" (He asked innocently).

"How dare you, are you trying to be funny?"

"No Sir, I couldn't help it, talking when you were, I mean."

"You're trying to make a fool of me, are you not, boy?"

"No, I wasn't, Sir."

"Come over here Armstrong, NOW." George walked slowly to the front of the class.

"Do you think History is boring or do you think I am boring, tell me are there any more at home like you?"

"Well, I have a younger brother he – Mr Ross immediately cut in, "I was being sarcastic you half-wit, what are you?"

"A half-wit, Sir."

"Well, you know what happens now, hands on the blackboard, palms flat and bend over." George began to cry, "please sir, no sir, I'm really sorry." Removing a thin cane from his desk Mr Ross struck the black-board with all his might, the loud noise filled the room. "DO IT NOW ARMSTRONG." George obeys, tears streaming down his face and on to the floor. The first stroke caused George to gasp in pain, then another and another, six in all. Normally he only gave three. "Now go back to you seat and stop that crying."

When George returned to his desk, he put his hands over his face. Jamie whispered, "Thank you for sparing me." When he lowered his hands, he was back in the empty classroom. So many days, so much bullying he thought.

Suddenly, downstairs he heard the boys leaving the hall. He left the room and headed for the stairs, halfway down he watched as the reception area started to fill up with the boys. Then he heard it, that voice, he gripped the bannister to stop himself shaking.

"Armstrong, what the hell are you doing?" bellowed Mr Ross. Riveted to the spot and without thinking he replied, "I have permission to be here, SIR." Everyone stopped talking and turned to look up at him.

George then realised he was addressing a boy named Armstrong. The silence ended and the boys started laughing and pointing at him. He sat down on the stairs feeling so stupid, that's enough he thought, this must end NOW. He rose went down the stairs and headed straight for Mr Ross. "You're Ross, aren't you? your flies are undone." All the boys started to laugh. "What, no, who are you?" he mumbled his face turning red. "My name is George Armstrong; I left this school in 1978." Ross shrugged and started to walk away saying, "Who cares?" George, who was tall grabbed the tubby little man by the scruff of his collar and pulled him back, there was a gasp from the audience. Other teachers came out of the hall and stood watching. "You're going nowhere shorty," As he held on to the now squirming man George noticed all the small faces were staring at him in silence, he spoke to them, "Do you know, when I was here, HE made us answer every question with Sir, does he still do that today?" A roar went up, yes he does. George continued, "He made my life a misery, he beat me, mocked, ridiculed, threatened and frightened me." He paused as he surveyed the young faces, Does he make anybody feel that way today?" Slowly a hand went up, then another, then lots of hands. "I thought so." He then let Ross go.

Earlier, hearing the commotion Joyce had come out of the office and stood next to the headmaster. They both heard everything.

The head walked forward, "Mr Ross please see me in my office at breaktime, now cut along boys, back to your classrooms."

When the reception area was empty the Head approached George, "Mr Armstrong, any future business with your company will no longer be required, good day to you." He then turned and walked away.

Joyce smiled at George saying, "Well done I can't stand Mr Ross he's always finding fault with my work, you've made my day." They shook hands and George left the school.

As he went through the front door he turned and saluted saying, "I lost their business, but it was worth it, closure at last."

LEGO

The countryside of West Sussex sped past the train as it headed for Brighton. Gavin Hunter sat back in his seat and thought of the two houses he was going to visit, one of which he would buy. Suddenly a passenger brushed past him, the young woman stopped and looked at Gavin, then bending down whispered in his ear, "It's in your pocket, I'll collect it when we reach Brighton, wait for me". She then moved on and through to the next carriage. How strange he thought as he felt in his pocket then brought out a red oblong piece of Lego, he examined it then shook it, nothing. Putting it back in his pocket and thought again of the two houses.

Gavin was a widower with three grown up children, none of them lived in the UK. He recently retired as a barrister and although he lived in Chichester, he always fancied living closer to the sea. The train pulled into Brighton Station; he remained seated as the passengers left the carriage. No sign of the woman. He stood on the platform for a while but still no mystery woman, so he continued with his day out.

On arriving home Gavin went into the kitchen to make a cup of coffee. Taking the phone from his pocket he felt the Lego, looking at it he smiled then threw it in the waste bin, crazy women he thought. A few days later Gavin was sat in the lounge watching the local new on TV when a picture of the mystery woman appeared. He sat bolt upright. Apparently, Sylvia Boothe private secretary to local MP Mark Sands has gone missing, CCTV showed the last sighting was of her leaving Brighton Station on her way home. She was reported missing by her husband Glen Boothe. Gavin rushed into the kitchen and emptied the waste bin over the floor and retrieved the Lego piece. After cleaning up he examined the piece again. This time he pushed each nodule separately, suddenly the end opened to expose a flash drive. He plugged it into his laptop – password required – damn it he thought. Shrugging off any thoughts of informing the police he made a phone call to a friend, an IT expert.

The following morning Gavin answered a knock on his front door "Hello Corky, come in", they went into the kitchen and opened the laptop, "You'll want to see this", said Corky.

Sylvia woke up and rubbed her eyes. The last thing she remembered was walking down the cul-de-sac where she lived and then being bundled into a Transit van. Looking around the beautifully decorated room she was puzzled, no restraints on her limbs and still in the clothes she was wearing last night. She stepped out of the bed she was on and went to the window, looking out she realised the room was on the top floor of a London hotel, she tried to open the room door, but it was locked. Giving up she went back to the bed and lay down. Moments later the door opened and a tall well-dressed young man entered the room, he pulled up a chair and sat down opposite the bed. "Good morning, Sylvia", he said. "Who the hell are you?", she replied. "I'm Jacob, a friend of Mark Sands – where's the flash drive?" She smiled, It's somewhere safe Jacob". He then explained the situation. "You've been delving into Mark's emails and private letters and found he had been falsifying expenses and syphoning off money from donations. You then put all your findings on to a flash-drive, very clever girl, why did you do it?" Sylvia swung her legs over the side of the bed and sat opposite from Jacob, "To expose him as a swindler of course". Jacob's face hardened, he leaned forward, "Are you going to give me the drive yes or no?" Her answer was swift, "NO". He leaned back, "let me fill you in on a few things, our IT man has been making a few alterations to your computer. So now it would appear that YOU are the swindler together with you lover".

Sylvia's faced dropped, she became worried, "Where's your proof?" "Just like you lady, on a flash drive, but there's more, I shall elaborate".

Before continuing he took a photo from his blazer pocket. "We are sitting in the penthouse suite of the Paragon Hotel Kensington that you have been renting for the past two weeks. The Doorman, the Concierge, and CCTV will confirm this". Jacob then shows her a photo. "You were seen coming and going, sometimes with a man". Sylvia grabbed the photograph, "that's not me". "Good likeness though, isn't it?" She was crestfallen, "The reason I didn't have the drive when you kidnapped me was because I dropped it in the pocket of a man on the train". Jacob became very angry, "you've got 48 hours to find it or all of this goes to the Press and the police, you're free to go".

Sylvia went straight home her husband was there, she told him some story about being kidnapped but it was a case of mistaken identity, so they let her go. She was kept blindfolded throughout. Glen believed her, it went no further.

Within 24 hours Sylvia had the flash drive. On returning to her office, she filled a box with her personal items, then, after writing a letter of resignation went into Mark Sands office. He looked up, "I think you've got something for me". "You first," said Sylvia. They exchanged drives, she then placed the letter on his desk, "my resignation", "good, I hope I never see you again, now get out". She returned to her office picked up the box and left the building. Mark sat back in his chair, I think all this went very well, he thought, I must thank Jacob for his help.

Gavin opened his front door, "Ah, Mrs Boothe, we meet at last, do come in". He closed the door, "I think you have come for the Lego piece", "correct, let me see it". He handed it to her, taking it, she asked if he had looked at, no he lied, anyone else see it, no he answered, lying again. Sylvia stared at him for a minute, "let me check if it's the one I gave you". He plugged in into his laptop and stood away from the screen. She opened the document, it showed Mark Sands office at 10pm, the blinds and door were closed.

Sands was embracing a very young Erin Scott, one of the office clerks, she then turned and bent over his desk, as he dropped his trousers Sylvia closed the document and removed the drive. She knew he was seeing Erin so placed a secret camera in his office. "Alright Gavin we need to have a little chat". Once they were seated in the lounge Sylvia told him the truth. She worked for MI5 as an undercover agent, she guessed there was a tail on her. After the Lego drop agents had followed Gavin, her kidnap was unexpected, she then apologised to him for the delay in getting back in touch. Gavin was amazed by all this, "don't worry I won't repeat a word to anyone". "Thank you" said Sylvia, as she produced an 'Official Secrets Act' form, "just sign this to be sure". She thanked him for his help, they shook hands and she left.

On reaching home, Sylvia, or Kate Dixon, her real name, began to unpack the box from the office. She laughed to herself, if Mark Sands only knew there were two flash drives instead of one. Out from the box she took a pen and pencil holder made of red Lego, a present from her little niece she told everyone. Two dummy pieces had been made for her, one of the two was part of the holder, it sat on her desk in plain sight all the time she was working for Sands.

The MP was arrested for fraud, he denied all charges and claimed he was an upright and honest husband and father. So, when the film of his adultery was passed to the media his credibility hit rock bottom.

FAREWELL

That's another success thought Robin as he left the Crown Court. As a criminal defence barrister, he was good and in great demand. As he turned left, he noticed a woman waving at him. It was his girlfriend, Liberty Squires, or Libby as she was known. "Over here Rob" she called. They kissed then got into Libby's mini-cooper and drove to the flat they shared in Ealing, London.

Their first meeting was three years ago when Libby was a defence witness at one of Robin's cases. At first, they chatted, then coffee, then dinner. She was a model and spent time in other countries on photo-shoots for anything from cars to cosmetics. Together they moved into the two-bedroom apartment. Libby's dad was a High Court judge with a country pile in the Cotswolds. The couple would often spend weekends there doing the usual things, shooting, or fishing. The only downside of their relationship was Robin liked a drink. He wasn't violent only silly or embarrassing. They had a good life together, until one night. The last weekend they stayed in the country went very well. Libby's parents were on great form. On the Sunday evening they set off for Ealing, Libby normally drove but she had sprained her ankle so Robin drove. During the weekend he hadn't appeared to drink much but what nobody knew he had a hip flask and would often swig from it when alone. They had travelled about three miles chatting and laughing when suddenly as the car rounded a bend Robin didn't see the tractor parked up on the grass verge until it was too late. The car swerved violently on the narrow county lane then skidded and ploughed straight into a tree. There was silence. Then Robin sat up "Libby, Libby, are you alright?" he shouted frantically. She was dead. Robins' life changed forever.

The first time he saw Libby's parents since the accident was at her funeral. He was on bail. Her father only spoke to him once, saying "I will be in touch. Two days later, as Robin left his flat, a black BMW stopped in front of him. Two men got out and bundled him into the car. A third man, sitting in the back held a chloroform-soaked pad across Robin's face until he passed out. He woke up in a large empty garage. He was tied to a chair with tape across his mouth. Three men stood in front of him their faces uncovered. Oh no, he thought, this doesn't look good. The man in the middle had a red scar across his forehead.

He took a mobile phone from his pocket, talked into it, then held it in front of Robin. What he saw was the face of the judge, Libby's dad. "Well Mr Myers" he said, "because of you my daughter is dead, justice must be done, this is the last time you will ever see me again, or indeed, anyone, so farewell". The man with the scar withdrew a gun from his waistband and shot Robin between the eyes. His body was found two days later in Epping Forest by a dog walker.

DCI Tom Waters and his Sergeant Jack Pellow stood looking down at the body. "So, what have we got Jack?" "Robin Myers guv aged 32". "Well, who would want him dead?" "Take your pick, guv, he was a lawyer". Tom fixed Jack with a look. "Sorry guv, Myers was drunk-driving last month, crashed the car, his girlfriend who was with him died. "Ah ha, said Tom, a motive". "Not if you're thinking of her dad, he's Judge Squires, High Court. The DCI thought for a moment, "OK Jack let's finish up here.

On the surface life for Sarah Mills was very rosy. She owned two successful nail bars. Alec, her car mechanic husband and her two children, Donna and Max lived happily in Bromley. Sarah, unfortunately, had a secret. She was a gambling addict, dogs, horses, cards, casino, betting shop or her laptop, she used them all. Sadly, her losses outweighed her winnings. Alec was totally unaware. She had taken out bank loans until they said, no more. Recently, in desperation, she borrowed from a loan shark.

One Friday she picked up the children from school and as a treat visited the local café for tea. As they finished their meal, a man sitting at the next table, turned to look at them. "Hello Sarah" he said. Donna looked at him and asked, "Do you know my mummy?" "Oh yes, we do business together" Max started laughing. "What's so funny?" asked the stranger. Max pointed at the man's face saying, "You look like Harry Potter". The man instinctively felt the red scar on his forehead "Nope, 'fraid not, I'm too old!" Pushing his chair back noisily he turned to Sarah "You've got 48 hours to settle up", then left the café. Before they could say anything, she rounded up the children saying, "Come on now let's go home".

Later that evening, sitting on the sofa with Alec, Sarah desperately wanted to tell him about her gambling, but she couldn't. two days later as Sarah was leaving the betting shop, the bullet hit her between the eyes, she fell down dead.

This second murder really bothered Tom as these latest shootings involved the same weapon as last year's murders, a Glock 19. Tom was assigned to that case. Although praised for his work the shooter was never caught. "I was this close" Tom was heard to say at the time.

Karl Robola, aged 19 and single, was a thief. He prowled the street coffee shops and cafés. Like a tiger hunting his prey, he moved silently. He stopped. A young woman was using her laptop. He moved closer while adjusting his face mask, thank God for covid he thought. Approaching the table, he looked at the ground "Is that your £5 note?" The woman looked up "Where?" He pointed, "There by the table leg". She bent down and looked under the table. Quick as a flash he slammed the laptop shut and ran with it under his arm. At a safe distance, into his shoulder bag it went. He continued his search and by the end of the day had stolen three mobile phones and a man's travelling bag, the sort you take on an aeroplane. The man had indeed arrived that morning in London from Paris. He was not a person to cross being the owner of a large security firm. He was able to access cctv anywhere in London. To Karl's delight the bag contained a wallet, passport, and a bottle of scotch. Everything else he dumped in a bin. Time to call it a day he thought as mounted his motor scooter.

Karl lived in a basement flat or 'garden flat' as the estate agent called it. The following day he took things easy and stayed indoors. Come night he was on his way to the 'Black Horse' pub. He parked up and waited for his next prey. About 30 minutes later a well-dressed man staggered out of the pub, as he reached his car, a Lexus, he put his hand on the roof to steady himself. The tiger pounced, he punched the man full in the face, he fell to the ground. Karl searched the man's pockets taking a wallet and phone but couldn't find the car keys. As he ran back and mounted his scooter the shot rang out. The car keys were in the Lexus, with the chauffeur.

The next day Tom Waters was in his office, deep in thought when in walked Sergeant Pellow "What's new guv?" he asked cheerfully. Ignoring him Tom went over to the evidence-board. "What was it that little boy in the café said?" he asked rhetorically pointing at the photo of the Mills family. "he said the nasty man at the next table had a red scar on his forehead. That boy is the only witness to have seen the shooter, apart from his sister".

Tom went back to his desk, sat down, and opened the file. He looked at Jack "The latest shooting, Karl Robola at the pub", he paused, "I know it's a long shot, but we should go back to the 'Black Horse' and check cctv footage of the car park from around 10pm, see if chummy was waiting in his car. "Come on Jack let's go.

The Real Estate trade has had its ups and downs, Freddy Fisher should know having been in the business for 30 years. He started as an Estate Agent and now owns three agencies of his own. Before she died his wife was the accountant. Recently he had decided to retire and let his two stepsons run the business. But something more serious was bothering him and that's why he had invited just his two daughters, Dawn, and Kay to visit.

It was noon on the Wednesday when the doorbell on Freddy's large, detached house in Beckenham, rang. Freddy kissed his daughters as they entered. "This is all a bit mysterious dad," said Dawn. Ignoring the remark Freddy ushered them into the garden where a barbeque was on the go. He poured three glasses of wine and handed one each to Dawn and Kay. As he picked up the third glass, he dropped it, the glass hit the ground and smashed. "Damn it shouted Freddy". "Don't worry Dad" said Kay, I'll clean it up, you go and check on the steaks". When the meal was over the family sat around the garden table drinking coffee. Freddy spoke, "Well girls I won't beat about the bush, I have a brain tumour. "Is it serious?" asked Dawn. "Yes, stage 4, I've probably got six months to a year" answered Freddy as he sipped his coffee. "I'm fine don't worry; I sometimes drop things but it's no big deal. Conversation continued until late afternoon.

After the girls had left, Freddy went into the sitting room and over to the drink's cabinet. He poured himself a large scotch and took a cigar from the humidor. Making his way to the armchair he sat down placing his glass on a small table beside him. He lit the cigar and took a few puffs. Feeling a bit woozy he put his hand to is head, his fingers passed lightly over the red scar on his forehead. He picked up his glass, raised it in the air saying out loud "To the Star Chamber, my paymasters – I thank you". As he went to take a sip the glass fell from his hand tipping the whisky over his chest, the shock made him drop the glowing cigar also onto his chest. "Dear God, no", he shouted. He could not move as the flames started.

Tom and Jack were at the 'Black Horse' looking at cctv footage of the car park. Sadly, nothing of any use. "Well, that's it, said Jack, lets go". "Not so fast matey". Tom turned to the landlord, "What have you got, inside the pub?" "We have two cameras', one facing the bar and one facing the room" Tom pointed at the screen "show us the room footage, say from 10.30pm". It showed the room was half empty. There was Mr Burton, the mugging victim sitting at a table chatting with two men. Close by was a man sitting at a table alone. "Stop there, said Tom, close up on that man". Both Tom and Jack gasped, they saw the red scar. "That's him said Tom, he must have followed Robola here knowing he was looking to score, Burton was the mark". With his phone Tom took a picture of the man and sent it to Greenside Police Station. He told them to check it with the Facial Recognition Unit.

The Landlord offered the Detective's lunch, they accepted. The reply came from Greenside, the man's name is Freddy Fisher. Previously he was in a street fight with one other male who cut him across the forehead with a stanley knife. Both men were arrested. Last known address as follows. Tom thanked the Landlord then turned to Jack "Set the satnav for Beckenham, we're on our way. When they arrived at Freddy's house there was no answer. When Tom looked through the front room window, he was shocked to see Fisher's chest on fire. Together they kicked the front door open and rushed into the sitting room. Jack grabbed a towel from the cloakroom and put out the fire which had only affected the chest and groin." Thank you" whispered Freddy. Tom stared at him, "Are you the shooter?" "Yes, you got me", he then pointed at the self portrait on the wall. "The safe". Those were Freddy's last words.

Jack pushed the painting to one side and stared at the wall safe "We need the password numbers". Tom stared at the painting, "I got it, look closely at the scar". Jack did, he noticed six small, twisted numbers 193118. He pushed the buttons and the safe door pinged open. Inside he found a stack of money a Glock 19 and a notebook, written on the cover it said 'Star Chamber Paymasters'. Tom phoned in their findings.

While they waited for backup Jack, while looking at his phone said, "Here guv this Star Chamber was a group of judges set up to make sure justice was done in the 15th century, sounds like a good idea to me, what do you think?"

Tom paused, "I don't think the judges actually paid hitmen to kill for justice". They both laughed.

ROBBERY

They say that during your last moments on earth your past life flashes before you, we don't know of course if that is true, but let's assume it is for Charlie Evans.

It was late November 1975, having finished breakfast, Charlie kissed his wife and two children goodbye and set off for the local Library where he worked. At around 11am two men entered separately and spoke to Charlie then followed him into the reading-room. They all sat together round a table. "OK Dave, weather for Friday?" asked Charlie. "Heavy rainfall all day", he replied. "Good, Norman, did you get a car?". "Yes boss, changed the plates this morning". "All right lads see you on Friday you know when. Dave and Norman left, and Charlie went back to work as the Librarian.

The rain was pouring non-stop as Charlie looked out of the window. He turned to his assistant. "Molly, I've got to catalogue some new books that have just come in, so I'll be busy in my office this afternoon, I don't want to be disturbed". "That's fine Mr Evans", she replied. At 2.45pm he put on his coat and hat grabbed his umbrella and left the library. It was Friday.

Just before 3pm, Dave and Norman were stood either side of the Northern Bank, Charlie approached, his face covered with a scarf and entered the Bank. The Manager was there, "I'm just about to lock up sir it's 3 o'clock". Dave and Norman moved swiftly and stood in front of the three cashiers, guns pointed. "Stand well back from the counter" shouted Norman , they obeyed. Charlie locked the bank door using the Managers keys then ordered him into his office. Before he locked him in, he cut the phone line. The cashiers were also put into the office, all were tied up and gagged and the door locked.

After forcing the Manager to open the vault they filled the three bags that Norman had brought and left. Norman drove the car and stopped at the back of the library and dropped off Charlie and the bags, then drove off with Dave. After hiding the cash in the basement, Charlie went back to work.

A police investigation found no witnesses, what with the heavy rain the few people that were around had umbrellas, nobody noticed anything. Over 5 years the trio robbed four more provincial banks; it was during the fifth robbery that things went wrong. George Downey the Manager was accidently shot "give me your scarf", shouted Charlie. He folded up the scarf and put it on the man's wound, telling the staff to keep the pressure on. He told them he would call an ambulance. The three robbers then took what money they could and left the bank. Unfortunately, when the ambulance arrived the Manager was dead.

Later they decided to stop the robberies, Norman went to live with his sister in Ireland and Dave moving to London. Charlie, well, he just went back to life as a Librarian. It wasn't long before Dave returned to crime. He was arrested for drug dealing and sentenced to 3 years in prison.

Life went on, 20 years down the line Charlie was now retired and had moved, together with his wife June, into a beautiful house in Devon. Norman, meanwhile, was still running the pub-restaurant in Kildare he had bought some years previously. Dave was in the wind. The three men had never contacted each other since splitting up in 1980.

The mid July sun shone brightly over the Devon coastline as Charlie sat in his conservatory reading a newspaper. Suddenly he was drawn to an article on page 15, it was headed 'The body of a 72-year-old man was found in London's East End'. He read on. The man identified as

David Moffatt was found stabbed to death in an alley off Munster Road Shoreditch. Police enquiries are ongoing. Charlie remembered Dave from all those years ago. Poor bloke he thought.

Kingfisher had just won the 2.30 at the Curragh Racecourse when Norman Carson nipped back to his car for his mobile phone. As he sat down a figure appeared behind him, he felt the point of a knife in his neck. "Should have locked the door Norman – your mistake".

Teresa, Norman's sister, began to worry, he had been gone for over 30 minutes, so she phoned him, it went to voicemail. Better go and see what's up, she thought. As she opened the driver's door, she saw the horror before her. Norman sat with his head down and the blade of a machete sticking out of his chest, it had been pushed through from the back of the seat to the front.

This story made the tabloids in the UK. On reading it Charlie was terrified. What's going on he thought, first Dave now Norman, we've not spoken in 20 years, who's doing this, are they coming for me? The answer came a week later in the form of a letter. On opening the envelope, written on the page was just two words 'You're Next'.

In 1990 DS Patmore was working on unsolved crimes, 'Cold Cases', dating back to the 1970's. He came across a bank robbery murder in 1980. The only physical evidence was a black scarf left behind by one of the three robbers. As DNA testing was now widespread, he sent it off for analysis. The results came back identifying David Moffatt. He was brought in for questioning. He admitted he was one of the three robbers but refused to name the other two. Of course, without the gun there was no way of proving who shot the Manager. He was later jailed for 5 years for robbery. Sitting in the press gallery during Moffatt's trial, was a reporter called Alex Downey. He bided his time. And when Dave was released, he followed him. Realising the old man was penniless and homeless he took him to a pub, bought him a drink the offered him £500 to name his friends. Dave took the money.

Using all his resources and contacts Downey tracked down Norman and Charlie. A week later he was on his way to Co Kildare, Ireland. The pub was easy to find. After having a meal there, he spent the evening at the bar chatting to Norman. Later in the B&B Downey laughed to himself, so we are all going horse-racing tomorrow.

Charlie resigned himself to his fate, what else can I do, he thought. One morning he went for a walk in the local park then sat down on a bench for a rest. The man who had been following also sat down on the bench. "Charles Evans?" "Yes, that's me". Downey moved closer. "A bank robber from the 1970's?". Charlie looked at the man, "Who ARE you?" "I am the son of the bank manager you shot; I killed your friends now it's your turn". He then plunged a knife into Charlie's chest. "We didn't kill anyone", whispered Charlie. "You did, one of you did." Charlie gathered his breathe, "one of the cashiers wrestled the gun from me then he accidently shot your dad, he later told the police it was one of us". Downey stood up then looked at Charlie for a moment, "I'm sorry", he said, then left the park.

The police stood around the park bench looking down at Charlie. Searching his pockets, they found a gun sealed in a plastic bag, also a mobile phone which had recorded the park bench conversation. Later Alex Downey was arrested for murder.

The last memories of Charlies past life were kissing his wife and children goodbye every morning before he set off to work – probably.

⸻⸻◈⸻⸻

LEO TAIT

It was lunchtime one Tuesday when Leo, head of Robotics at the Pharmacon Institute, walked out never to return. He had a plan. The first thing he did on entering his apartment in west London was to open his laptop and effortlessly transfer £1,000,000 from the Institute to a secret overseas bank account. He then bought a plane ticket to Russia and left the UK later the same day using a forged passport.

The Institute existed solely to help the disabled. Using state of the art technology and the finest technicians they produced artificial limbs. There was also a pharmaceuticals department and a Robotics department. It wasn't until the Wednesday that all hell broke loose. The CEO, Russell Danvers, convened a special board meeting. "What the hell's going on, 1 million goes missing along with our top man in Robotics, any answers, anybody?" No one spoke. "For now, he continued, we keep this to ourselves, no police press or publicity, he then pointed at Melina Crouch, you're head of IT, see what you can find out, right, back to work everyone."

Two weeks after he left Leo returned to the UK and rented a house in South London. He now started to put his plan into action. Liam Smiley who worked with Leo received the phone call he was expecting. For about a year he had worked with Leo in an underground laboratory perfecting their own robot. The call summoned him urgently to the Lab.

Around 7pm Melinda drove into her parking space in front of the block of flats where she lived. As she got out of the car a man dressed in black appeared and stabbed her through the heart. He took her handbag and mobile phone then drove off in her car. Another tenant parking his car found her and called the police. It was classed as a mugging pending further investigations. The car was later found near a graveyard in Croydon. The police then visited the Institute and spoke to Russell Danvers, he could no longer keep things a secret and told them everything. Leo Tait then became a 'person of interest'.

When Liam entered the Lab and met with Leo, he was very angry. "What the hell's going on, I know you murdered Melinda, why?" "Look Liam she was top IT expert and may have found things out about us, I could not take that risk." "Well, count me out Leo I never agreed to murder." "I'm sorry to hear that Liam but as we've now completed our work, I no longer need you," without a flicker of emotion he grabbed Liam by the throat and strangled him to death. He later disposed of the body.

Mr Danvers always arrived for work an hour before anyone else, he liked the peace and quiet to check over the previous day's events. He hung up his coat then sat down at his desk. On hearing the door of his private cloakroom open, he looked round and saw Leo. "Good God man what's going on, where have you been?" Leo locked the office door and closed the blinds he then sat down opposite Russell. "I have started my own business," he said, adjusting his tie. "But you belong here, your work is important." "Well Russ I don't agree with your philanthropy, this whole helping the disabled thing, it's not for me." Russell gasped, "You are the most advanced robot technician in the world." Totally calm Leo replied, "I know I am, but I want fame and wealth, things I won't get working here so I've built a male robot, it's not like the one's here, he paused, mine is programmed to kill. A soldier of war, just one is equal to ten or more ordinary soldiers, many countries will pay a fortune for this." Russell looked at Leo, "so what do you want from me?" "I want you to forget me, never mention my name again to anyone, press, media or police, if you do, I will kill you. "He then unlocked the office door. "I was never here, OK?" Russell nodded, "you were never here."

As Russell was thinking over the talk with Leo, his secretary knocked and entered, "your coffee Mr Danvers." "Thank you, June." As she reached the office door she turned, "oh, I've been told to tell you that Mr Smiley hasn't been seen since yesterday and he's not answering his phone either." "Thank you, June."

As he sat at the head of the boardroom table, he told the members of his meeting with Leo. The idea that a super-weapon would soon be available to the highest bidder, military or non-military even, appalled them. They then discussed the absence of Liam Smiley, was he involved? It was decided that Russell and two members of security would search Liam's house for any evidence of his involvement.

Leo had returned to his underground Laboratory. Next to it was a bunker, a large empty space in which he set to arranging a display to be seen on his dark web site. Streaming would begin in 3 hours. He then waited for two Russian agents to arrive. They worked for the GRU, Military Intelligence, part of the KGB.

Russell entered Liam's house and began searching for evidence. No laptop was found, he must carry it with him thought Russell, they found nothing, files or dossiers. They were about to leave when one of the security men called out, "what about this?" In one of the desk drawers he'd found a document headed 'Mannequin Models', it was a sales receipt for the purchase of premises in a retail park in Mitcham. Russell read it; this must be a cover for Leo's laboratory he thought.

The officer in charge of the Crouch murder, DI Roberts, answered his phone, he spoke to Mr Danvers who asked him to come and see him at the Institute urgently as he had new evidence. He left immediately. On arriving at Pharmacon he was shown into the CEO's office. Russell stood up and shook hands with DI Roberts, "thank you so much for coming, please take a seat." "So, what's so urgent Mr Danvers?" As he sat down, Russell showed him the document, "I think this is where Leo is working from." "OK, I'll phone for back-up and we'll pay him a visit."

"Before you do Detective, there's something I have to tell you about Leo." DI Roberts leaned forward, "carry on." "He is not the man you think he is, my team and I made him, at the time it was the most advanced robot ever made, we named him Leo Tait which stands for Tomorrows Artificial Intelligence Today, a touch of vanity I grant you. He has, in secret, been building his own A.I except this one is programmed to kill, and Leo intends to sell a batch of them to anyone who will pay. As he told me he is only seeking wealth." Roberts gasped, "so if we find him he may kill me and my back-up, if that what you're saying what should we do?" "Let me come with you, said Russell, I think I can help." "Only if you are sure." "I'm sure Detective, shall we go?"

Inside the warehouse Leo was explaining to the Russians about the display, the robot, now dressed in army fatigues and holding a semi-automatic rifle containing blanks would seek out the two men who would be hiding behind various tall blocks of wood dotted around the bunker, their weapons contained live ammunition. Suddenly the warehouse alarm sounded, the three men made there way to the office upstairs and checked the cctv. DI Roberts walked towards the warehouse door his back-up followed behind. The door opened and out stepped the three men, the Russians had their hand up, we innocent men they shouted. "OK said the DI, so jog on." The Russians just looked at him. "Go, clear off." They ran. Leo then took his phone from his pocket and pressed the screen, the warehouse door opened and the soldier appeared, he looks just like an ordinary bloke thought Roberts. The robot raised his rifle, now loaded with live rounds. Either leave now or all of you will be dead within 30 seconds. Nobody moved. "Have it your own way," he said he raised his phone, wonderful things APPS aren't they." He touched the screen, saying 'that's stage 1 activated.' Still nobody moved. He went to touch it again when his body went rigid, and he fell like a tree in a forest.

Russell walked forward from behind the police van, "yes, apps ARE wonderful," he said. "What the hell did you do?" asked Roberts. "Well, it was a gamble I know, but during the construction of Leo I build in a safety programme in case he turned rogue, which he did," he held up his iPhone, it's a 'Kill' button, I've never had to use it, so it was a gamble." Roberts looked at the soldier, "What about him?" Russell told him he was harmless without instructions, he asked for both A.I's to be brought to the Institute where he would dismantle them.

Between the Lab and the bunker was a room which contained ten-armed robot soldiers, they stood in two rows of five, their eyes closed. Suddenly Leo's voice could be heard from a speaker attached to one wall. 'Hear me, hear me, their eyes opened, stage 1 is now activated, proceed with your mission after the countdown. 10-9-8-7-6 -5. . . . .

THORNBUSH ISLAND

Day One.

The July sun was hot and the water almost still as the small motorboat chugged its way towards Thornbush, a small uninhabited island. Inside the boat sat the Langford family Dean, Dot and their two boys Noah,12, and Brian, 14. They were visiting the island for a four-day camping holiday. On arrival Dad secured the boat against the small jetty. Everyone helped to unload the contents and then set off seeking a place to set up camp. They found the perfect spot in a glade among the trees. Mum and Dad erected the tents while the boys went in search of firewood for the evening fire. The chores done Dean set up the little gas stove to heat up the beef stew Dot had made that morning. After dinner the fire was lit and all sat around chatting and toasting marshmallows. "Are you having fun boys?" asked Dot. "Yes mum, said Noah, it's a bit like ' swallows and amazons." "Well lads, it's time for bed," said Dean. When the boys were tucked up in their tent Dean and Dot sat by the fire with a glass of wine. There was silence at first, just the hooting of a nearby owl. "We're ok now, aren't we Dot?" She turned to look at him, "yes my darling we are, she replied as she stroked his face, I remember what happened when we were here all those years ago." Dean smiled, "do you mean when I asked you to marry me?" he replied sheepishly. "Yes, my love I do." They kissed.

When they married, Dean was a Police Constable. He threw himself into the job, worked all hours plus overtime when he could get it so he could earn enough to buy a house. Dot was a nurse and did the same. It was alright at first, but when the boys came along things changed. Dean was promoted to Sergeant but carried on working all hours. Dot saw less and less of him, they argued, both were unhappy.

Their future became uncertain, but Dean 'saw the light' as it were and he changed. Things got better. This holiday was part of that change.

Day two.

It was a beautiful sunny morning as the family sat around the table eating breakfast. "So, what do you want to do this morning boys," asked Dean. "Bullseye," shouted Noah "Of course, he replied, I noticed you'd brought your bow and arrows." Brian then fetched the game from his tent. The bow was bigger than a toyshop variety and the arrows were longer but still had the suckers on the ends. He attached the bullseye picture card to a tree using drawing pins. Both boys then took it in turns to hit the bullseye. Mum and Dad watched for a bit then decided to go for a quick swim in the lake.

In the afternoon, after lunch they all went for a walk, Brian brought his metal detector. Every so often he was asked, 'anything yet?' The answer was always, 'not so far.' They ventured about half a mile from camp, then, as they made their way back Brian suddenly shouted that he had found something. Standing beside him they all heard the rapid beep beep from the detector, using his trowel Brian dug the earth away until he hit something solid, Noah helped using his hands. What they hauled out of the ground was a black metal box about 16 inches square by 12 inches deep with handles on two sides. Dean got down on his knees undid the metal clasps and opened the lid. "Wow," said the boys, buried treasure." It was full of plastic sleeves each one containing a wad of £50 notes. Dean slammed the lid shut. After the boys filled in the hole, they returned to camp with the box. The boys wanted to count the money but Dot said that wasn't important, they need to find who it belongs to, she gave them a 'bag for life' telling them to fill it with firewood . When they had gone Dean looked at Dot, "There's something very dodgy here," "I agree she replied." They counted the cash, there were 20 sleeves each worth £2,000 , £40,000 in all. They put the money into one of their bigger holdalls. The box was put in the corner of the tent for fingerprint identification as Dean put it. Dinner that evening was very lively, talk of buried treasure, who owned it, was it a long dead pirate, and so on.

Day Three.

Dot woke up, yawned, and rubbed her eyes, "what'll we do today then." She looked across at Dean, but his bed was empty. Trying not to panic she left the tent; the boys were already up and eating their cereal. She told them Dad was missing, he must have gone back to the mainland as there was no mobile signal on the island. "If he has gone back then he must have taken the boat, said Brian, shall we have a look?" "Ok, replied Dot, let's go." The boat had indeed gone. As they returned to camp the sound of a motorboat could be heard, they went back to the shoreline, "must be Daddy coming back," said Noah. Dot could see it wasn't. "Quick boys I think they're bad men, run." Back at camp they grabbed warm coats and fled into the woods.

The boat docked at the jetty, two armed men got out and headed for the hidden metal box. They were surprised to see the camp, as they searched the tents the empty box was found. They guessed it was a family, 2 adults and 2 kids. If there was no luck finding them on the island it would mean they left for the mainland. They started to search. After about an hour the men found them, "right, back to camp", said the man called Andy. When they reached the clearing, the other man, Harry, made them sit down. Andy spoke, "where's the cash?" "I don't know, said Dot, it's probably on the mainland by now with my husband." "So why didn't you all go with him?" "Because we're on holiday and we didn't know you were here, stupid." The man was angry now, "well, you've seen our faces so we will have to shoot you all." The boys burst into tears.

"You first, lady." "No, Andy shouted Harry, we're not murderers." Andy raised his gun and pointed it at Dot, just then there was a noise by the trees, he looked up, the last thing he saw was an arrow heading towards him. The arrow had no sucker, but the end was sharpened into a spike, it went through his eye and into his brain. He was dead before he hit the ground. Harry dropped his gun and ran. Dean stepped forward still holding the bow. They all hugged, "I'll explain everything later, he said, but first we have to go back to the mainland." Once aboard the boat they saw Harry in his boat, it was sinking. "Sorry about that, said Dean, smiling." They hauled him aboard, then phoned the police and explained everything and requested an ambulance.

Day 4.

The family were now back at home. After a long lie-in they were sat together eating breakfast still in their pyjamas. Dean filled them in about the events of yesterday. He left the tent early took the money and the bow and arrows and drove the boat to the other side of the island. He knew someone would come for the box, 'coppers instinct' he called it. He knew if he'd stayed with the family, they would all be in jeopardy, so he watched them from a distance until he saw his chance to strike back. The money was from drug dealing then laundered, the 'clean' money was then hidden on the island ready to be collected by Andy and Harry. The family were just in the wrong place at the wrong time. Dean was worried about the boy's mental health after everything that had gone on, "how are feeling," he asked them. "You won the game," said Brian, excitedly. "I don't understand," he replied, "You scored a bullseye," he shouted as he punched the air. No problem there thought Dean, relieved. "OK lads off you go and get dressed." The boys left the room. "How many sleeves do you have," Dot asked and winked. "I've got 2 sleeves my love," he replied and winked back at her.

LIFE OF MAGIC

As he sat in his father's study Myles looked at the framed poster on the wall, it was headed ' Marco & Son – Magic and fun for everyone'. It was dated July 1977. His father had recently died of cancer. His funeral, earlier that day was, let's say, different from the normal.

Marco had pre-recorded a message which was then played during the service at the crematorium. 'Thank you everyone for coming today, this being my last ever show. This room is a bit like a theatre, all of you sitting in the front stalls and me in a box. I was always very good at escapology, but this is one routine I can't escape from. I do hope my son Myles carries on the family business of magic. I love you all and bid you farewell.' There were a few snuffles from the mourners. When it came for the curtain to close in front of the coffin the room was filled with the sound of the London Symphony Orchestra's version of The Final Countdown by Europa.

Myles thoughts went back to the early days when the posters read 'Marco & Maria – Magic and Illusion'. All that changed when his mother, Maria, walked out leaving a note saying she wanted to start a new life abroad. He was 12 years old, he never saw her again.

There was a knock on the study door and Myles wife entered, "it's getting late darling, time we were going home." They went downstairs and joined their two daughters, Anna and Sadie. "Where have you been Daddy?" asked Sadie. "Oh, just in Granddad's study." Anna, the younger girl hugged him round the waist saying, "are you still sad Daddy?" He smiled, not so much, now that I've seen the lovely faces of all my girls." He clapped his hands, "now get your coats on or I'll make you disappear." They all laughed.

That evening, after the children were in bed, Jenny asked Myles about his father's house. "Do you really want to sell it, or would you like us to move in there, after all it's where you grew up?"

Marco was born in 1938. By 1965 he was married with one son and working as an insurance salesman in London. One lunch time he was wandering around Covent Garden when he came across the famous Percy Press in the middle of his Punch & Judy show. This moment was to change Marco's life forever. He was fascinated by the simple comedy and the laughter of the children watching the show. This is what I want to do, he thought.

That weekend he started to build a puppet booth. Later buying a set of puppets and a 'swazzle' (to create Punch's distinctive voice). He wrote a script and a month later all was ready. He visited the Head of his son's Infant School and offered to do a free Punch & Judy show. She was delighted and suggested the following Friday at 11.30am.

Marco was very nervous as he set up the booth in the school hall. As the children trooped in, his son saw him and waved. The show went down very well, he loved doing it, but more importantly, the children loved it.

Soon bookings for birthday parties started to come in, the word had spread. To extend the show he added some magic trick, plate spinning and balloon animals, there was one for each child to take home. He then advertised in the local press and more bookings followed.

After three years Marco decided to change the show, to go upmarket. He discussed his ideas which included Maria as part of the act. She agreed, so the Marco & Maria – Magic and Illusion Act was born. They hired an Agent and went professional. Selling insurance was now over! They toured theatres and seaside resorts while Myles was looked after by a nanny. During the school holidays he came with them. The act now included escapology, juggling and balancing. They became very successful.

99

The act came to an end in 1976 when Maria left. Marco was heartbroken, he retired and stayed at home to look after his grieving son. Eight months later the idea of a father and son act was discussed. It would be a children's show again but only during school holidays. A choice of puppet shows was now available, Punch & Judy, Little Red Riding Hood or 3 Little Pigs. Marco wrote several comedy routines for the two of them. One was called 'The Chinese Washing Machine', they dressed up as Ping Pong from Hong Kong and Pong Ping from Beijing. Another was Marco making a balloon mouse and giving it to Myles who promptly threw it on the floor and stamped on it. "What did you do that for?" "It was a rat." "Oh no it wasn't." "Oh yes it was." and so on with the audience joining in. The children loved the anarchy.

What Marco and Myles loved most of all was at the end of a show when they said, 'Goodbye boys and girls, goodbye', the children would say 'Oh, no' or 'Please don't go'. This was better than money, any day.

A week after the funeral Myles returned to his father's house. He was in the study again only this time he was sorting through all the papers and documents. In one of the desks drawers, he found an envelope, it was addressed to him it said, If I don't get better – read this letter. He opened it and read.

Dear Myles,

If you are reading this letter, I must be dead. I have kept a dark secret for so long I now want to share it with you. It happened one weekend when you were staying with your Auntie Joan. I was busy in my workshop building a new illusion called 'The Vanishing'. I had finished making the oblong box that Mum would vanish from. She got into it and laid down, I wanted to make sure she was comfortable. I then closed and secured the lid and moved behind the box, but I tripped and fell banging my head on one of the props. I was unconscious and didn't wake up until the following morning. I rushed to open the box, but Mum was dead, she had suffocated.

You can imagine how I felt. In a blind panic I buried my beautiful wife in the garden by the acer tree. I then wrote that letter. Dear God, why didn't I just call an ambulance. I am truly sorry for not telling you sooner. Mum did not leave you, she loved you so much. Please forgive me Myles.

Your loving Father, Marco.

He read the letter again then sat quietly as the tears fell. Why didn't you tell me, he thought, we told each other everything, the two of us were so close.

Myles had not carried on the family business of magic as his father had hoped. He had joined the Police Force instead and was now a Detective Sergeant. After returning to work he showed the letter to his Inspector. Myles no longer wished to live in his fathers house, a few days later he sold it.

⊷⊶⊰◆⊱⊷⊶

ALL EYES AND EARS

As he stood in front of the mirror adjusting his tie, 18-year-old Roy felt very nervous, it was his first day as an Enquiry Agent with the Sheldon Agency. He got the job as his dad (a policeman) used to work with Jim Sheldon before he retired and started the detective agency. As Roy buttoned up the jacket on his dark blue Burton's suit, he decided that 1966 was going to be his best year yet.

After a short walk from his newly rented bedsit in Putney – his family home was in Bromley, too far to travel every day – Roy arrived at the office and rang the doorbell. The door was opened by Mr Regan the Office Manager, "Ah, you must be Roy, follow me." They went up the stairs then turned left down a corridor. "That's Interview room 1 said Regan, pointing and that's interview room 2 and here's Mr Sheldon's office." They knocked and entered. "Please sit down said Sheldon, I'll come straight to the point, you are here on a month's trial, if you succeed, you're in if not you're out, OK?" "Yes sir."

At the end of the corridor was a large square room with 3 desks up against one wall and 3 against another, in the middle stood a large table. As they entered, the staff turned to look. "This is Roy said Mr Regan, introduce yourselves," he then left the room. One of the men stood up, "my name's Rex but you can call me T, that's Betty but call her Boo." Then a rather tubby man stood up, "my name is Billy, but you can call me" - Roy interrupted him – "Don't tell me , It's Bunter, am I right? " "Er... no it's Bill." Rex quickly continued, "O-K, they are the agents, and these two lovely ladies are the secretaries, Dervla (she nodded at Roy) and Clara, she's French." She smiled at Roy saying,

"Bonjour monsieur, you are a pretty boy." He blushed and replied, "Bonjour, comment tale vous?" "Oo la la, you speak French?" "Well, a little, un peu." "I like you; you can be my toyRoy." Rex then spoke up, "And, moving on, last but not least, over there by the switchboard is young Hattie."

"So, what's your full name then," asked Billy." "It's Roy Rogers, actually." A small ripple went round the room. "Really, your dad must have a sense of humour, I think we'll call you cowboy, everyone agree?" Yes, came the answer.

"This empty desk here will be yours," said Rex, Roy went over to it, "What happened to the previous agent?" he asked. "You don't want to know replied Rex, then added, do you carry a knife?" "No," "Pity."

For the first week Roy had to remain in the office, sorting the post, that's what the big table was for, and answering the enquiries that Hattie put through to his phone, agents that were in the office would help him. He was happily sorting the post when his phone rang. Hattie was dealing with another caller, so she put the call straight through to Roy. "Hello, can I help?" "Yes, came a stern reply, ask Mr Sheldon to phone the Commissioner at 3pm, got it?" said the caller rudely. "Yes sir, replied Roy, Mr Sheldon to call the commissionaire at 3pm." "No, you fool, a commissionaire is a man in uniform outside a hotel, the Commissioner is the head of the Metropolitan Police." Now flustered Roy replied, sorry sir, I've made a note – 3pm. The caller rang off.

The week went well for Roy except for one phone call.

"Hello, can I help?"

"My name is Mrs Beattie, and my boy Kim is missing."

"I think that a job for the police, Mrs Beattie."

"I spoke to them 3 days ago, but they haven't come back to me."

"How old is Kim and what happened."

"He's 7 years old. I didn't close the front door tight, and he wandered off. I've pinned posters to the trees in my street, with his picture on, I thought that might help."

(A pause). "Tell me Mrs Beattie, is Kim a dog or a cat?"

"My lovely boy is a Yorkshire terrier."

"I'll tell you what to do, phone the RSPCA and tell them, they will help you, I'm sure."

"I'll do that, thank you so much for your help, goodbye."

Roy banged the desk with his fist, "how could I be so stupid." Rex was listening in on the extension, "no mate you did good, you didn't laugh you advised her, you helped her, well done." "Thank you T."

9.30 Monday morning and everyone is working except Clara, suddenly the door bursts open and in she runs, "so sorry, I overslept, my clock didn't go ping ping." She quickly took off her coat and sat down not realising she'd forgotten to put a skirt on. The fellas stared, such tiny panties, thought Roy. Dervla went over and whispered in her ear, the word 'merde' was heard by all. Carla rushed over to the hat stand and put her coat back on and kept it on all day.

"Alright lads, eyes back in their sockets, said Rex, let's talk about this week." The assignment was for three of them to attend at Ascot racecourse for Royal Ascot week. Betty, Roy, and Rex would go undercover to find illegal tipsters and, with the help of security, evict them.

Roy had no interest in horse racing, so concentrated on his job. The first race was at 2.30pm – The Queen Anne Stakes, he watched it with mild interest. Later, while looking at his programme, a man came up to him and grabbed the programme and scribbled something in it, he handed it back saying 'there you go chief, that'll be 5 bob. Roy showed the man his Security Pass saying, "You'd better come with me." The man disappeared into the crowd. Roy looked at what the tipster had written, he had circled 'Celtic Song' to win. It didn't.

Every lunchtime they all went to Rex's Auntie, who lived nearby, for a meal. By Wednesday she noticed Roy always took his shoes off and rubbed his feet. " Everything alright she asked." "I'll be ok." She picked up one of his shoes, "no wonder you're in pain," she said waving it at him. "That's the latest fashion, he replied, Cuban heeled boots like The Beatles wear." She smiled and fetched a pair of her husband's shoes.

The last race on Saturday was at 5.30pm – The St. James Palace stakes. At last, it's all over thought Roy. He did catch some tipsters during the week though, so that cheered him up. What he did enjoy was using his pass to visit both enclosures – The Silver Ring and the Royal enclosure, the latter only for people with invites. Also, he was glad to see the Royal Family close up in their horse drawn carriage.

Week 3 brought some interesting outings for Roy. He only had to work on Monday morning as Monday night he had an assignment with Betty. The morning job was to serve divorce papers on Douglas Bell. His eyes lit up when he realised Bell was the lead singer of the pop group 'The Majors'. They would be rehearsing at the Barons Club in London. The front door was locked, so he waited by the back door. A cleaner later emerged with waste baskets to empty, Roy darted into the building and headed for the stage. He waited for a while as the band went through their playlist. He suddenly realised he was there to do a job. As he walked across the stage the four-piece band stopped playing and looked at him. "Top marks for getting in here mate," said Dougie, I guess it's autographs you want." "No actually, only yours on these divorce papers." The band roared with laughter, and Roy couldn't help smiling. "You are one cheeky bastard, said Dougie,but anyway, would you like one of these?" He held up a signed photo of the band. "Blimey, yes please." He then shook hands with each band member, and as he left the stage Dougie shouted after him, "buy a ticket next time."

At 7pm on the dot than evening the beep-beep of a car horn sounded outside Roy's bedsit. He rushed outside and got into Betty's A35. Their job was to visit several 'BurgerBun' restaurants as secret shoppers and to report on everything from food quality to the manners of the staff.

Roy was looking forward to this one to one with Betty. A chance to just talk, he admired her no-nonsense attitude. As they sat in the first of five restaurants Roy learnt that Betty was 28 a former soldier and police officer before she joined the agency. She found the duties of a WPC to be too menial, never being in the front line, so she left. He told her all about himself. They became firm friends.

Roy should have paced himself, but the chance of free food was too much, by the time they reached the fifth place he was feeling decidedly bloated. After he'd paid the bill Betty was already out the door and heading for the car, as he ran to catch up with her, he saw a man, his hands all over her, he stopped not knowing what to do. Betty wasn't having any of it, she forced the man's arm up his back then grabbed him round the throat and threw him on the ground then kicked him in the stomach saying, "now piss off unless you want some more." He got up and limped away. Turning to Roy she said, "that bloke wants to learn some better chat-up lines." They both laughed as they got in the car.

The next morning Roy and Betty didn't have to be in work until 1pm, They spent the afternoon writing up their restaurant reports ready to be typed. As they were leaving the office after work, Dervla and Clara asked Roy if he wanted to go with them to 'The Swan' pub, he said yes. After a few drinks Dervla said she had to go home. He and Clara had a couple more also a club sandwich. As they left the pub Roy asked Clara if she lived very far way. "Not far, you want to walk me home?" Roy said yes, so they linked arms and set off. "This is where I live, do you want to come in for coffee, my toyroy," she was a bit tipsy.

"Toyboy? I don't think so, I'm 18 and your 21, yes, coffee, lovely." Clara, like Roy, lived in a bedsit, she boiled the kettle and made coffee. "Come and sit next to me on the bed, mon cheri," she said seductively. Let's just say a lovely time was had by all!

Roy spent the next few days in the office. Clients regularly sent over possible new employee CV's to be checked out so most of the day was spent on the phone.

And then the day came for the last assignment of his 4-week trial. He was to take a package to a Mr Mancini at the Hilton Hotel.

On his arrival he went to reception and asked for Mr Mancini. A few minutes later two men in dark suits approached and asked him to follow them. On the 5th floor they walked down the corridor and knocked on room 5023. The door opened and Roy entered, the two men stayed outside. An old man sitting behind a walnut writing bureau waved at Roy to come forward, "Buongiorno," he said as he stretched his hand out, Roy gave him the package, "grazie," he added, then waved Roy away saying, "puoi andare – you may go." Roy went to the suite door then turned and said, "arrivederci." The old man smiled.

What Roy learnt later was, at that time, no one was allowed to bring more that a certain amount of cash into the UK. The package contained cash, a loan for Mr Mancini who, incidentally, was believed to be Mafia connected. The Sheldon Agency was later repaid plus a fee. Business is business.

Mr Sheldon finished reading the file and looked up at Roy sitting opposite him. "Well, you have a glowing report from everyone, except one he said with a serious look on his face, any idea who that might be?" Roy swallowed hard, "no sir, no idea who." Sheldon sat back in his chair. "Well, I'll tell you and put you out of your misery, he paused for moment, it's Martha the cleaner, you keep leaving your teacup on your desk instead of in the sink." He then roared with laughter, you can stay with the Agency, cowboy, if you want to." he put out his hand, Roy shook it saying, "thank you sir, thank you, I won't let you down I promise." "Good man, now off you go."

As Roy entered the main office a big cheer went up and everyone clapped. He made a short speech thanking them for their help and their friendship. Someone then opened a bottle of bubbly, and they all drank a toast to the 'cowboy'.

When he got home, Roy rang his mum and dad and told them the news, they of course were very pleased. As he replaced the receiver, he thought to himself, 1966 is definitely going to be my best year ever.

THE BUNGALOW

The car showroom was very busy that morning, 21year old Dylan Parker had just sold his third car. "Another satisfied customer", he said to Moira who worked on the reception desk. The couple had been engaged for 6 months and both lived with their parents as they saved for a house deposit. "Lunch? asked Moira looking at her watch, It's 12.30". "Can do", he replied.

Dylan had worked at the car showroom for the past 3 years, he was a popular and successful salesman, he actually cared for his customers. Moira had started working there on her 18th birthday, 2 years ago.

Moving on a year Dylan had been promoted to Sales Manager, not long after that they were married. After a two-week honeymoon in Cornwall, they move into their new home, a two-bed detached bungalow. They were in love and happy.

After six months they were even happier with the arrival of their daughter, Maisie. Ever since she could walk Maisie would skip into her parents bedroom at 10am every week-end and jump on the bed saying "Wake up sleepy heads." "We are awake", they replied. She would then run and wait by the bedroom door saying, "Come on then, time for breakfast". Dylan and Moira kissed, donned their dressing gowns and the trio headed for the kitchen at the other end of the bungalow.

On one particular Saturday at 10am Maisie ran into the bedroom and jumped on the bed saying, "Wake up sleepy heads". "We are awake." "Today is my 7th birthday." "We know it is." Maisie giggled, "Are you taking me somewhere nice where I've never been before?" "Yes, we are, said Moira, off the bed now, time for breakfast." The three of them then made their way to the kitchen.

109

Moira and Maisie were sitting at the table when Dylan turned on the gas cooker. The blast was heard by the whole street.

The Fire Brigade arrived and put out the fire, only half of the bungalow had collapsed, the bedrooms were still standing. The cause of the blast was later confirmed as a gas leak. An ambulance took away the three bodies.

The site was fenced off by the Fire Brigade. Tearful neighbours visited and left flowers, cards, and cuddly toys against the fence. it was a clear indication that the Parker family were well loved.

On the Sunday at 10am, the day after the blast, Maisie ran into the bedroom and jumped on the bed, "Wake up sleepy heads." "We are awake." Maisie jumped off the bed, "Come on, time for breakfast. She ran to the bedroom door and waited. As the trio left the bedroom they vanished. This scenario played out every morning at 10am until the following Saturday.

The site was bought by a property developer who intended to clear the site and build a new house. The demolition squad arrived on the Saturday morning.

On 10am that morning Maisie jumped on the bed, "Wake up sleepy heads." "We are awake." "Today is my birthday, are you taking me somewhere nice where I've never been before?" "Yes, my darling, it will be heavenly." As the trio left the room they vanished – forever.

HOLIDAY GETAWAY

The Oxford was a popular restaurant in London's West End as Harry Bullen noticed as he walked between the tables towards the owner's office at the back. "Come in Harry, take a seat," said Marcus Bloom.

"I just popped in to say your payment went through ok and your order is on its way, the ship docks in Liverpool in two days." Marcus smiled, "that's good news." Harry stood up to leave. "Well, I've never let you down before, have I?" "No son, you haven't."

The National Crime Agency and armed police were in hiding at the Liverpool docks waiting for the ship to arrive. Also watching was an unmarked black van parked nearby. As the crew stepped off the boat the police ran forward and arrested them. The ship was searched by the NCA, they found drugs and weapons. The van drove away unseen.

That evening at Archway Police Station the phone rang in the CID office. Detective Rollins answered it. "The calls for you Gov," he handed the phone to DI Harry Bullen. "Harry, Telford here, just wanted to tell you the good news, we got 'em." "Got who, Rory?" "The Liverpool mob of course." Harry gasped and sat down. "This raid should have gone through me, you know that" said Harry loudly "I know, but the last three times they were always one step ahead of you, so we had to do this one on the QT. To be honest Harry we think you've got a mole in your office. Anyway, gotta go, speak soon." He hung up.

Marcus was in his restaurant office when he got the call from the men in the black van, he was furious, "get back here now." He then phoned his business partner and told him their shipment had been taken by the police. "We're two mill down, find Harry Bullen, search his flat, do whatever it takes but find him and bring him to me."

What nobody knew was that the NCA had an undercover officer working for the Liverpool mob, so they too were looking for Bullen.

Two days later Marcus got the news he was waiting for, Bullen was in Sorrento in Italy, staying at the Nizza Hotel. He sent a team to fetch him. The NCA through intel had also learnt of Bullen's whereabouts.

Russ and his wife Poppy were sunbathing by the pool of the Carlton Hotel in the holiday resort of Sorrento. Russ's watch pinged, he sat up, "Poppy honey, it's time to get ready for the coach outing."

The coach made its way up the coast, the first stop was Positano then on to Amalfi. The couple took a leisurely stroll around the town. After visiting the Cathedral, they went for afternoon tea at a little café. They forgot the coach was about to leave, rushing to the parking lot they saw it driving away. "Damn, said Russ, what do we do now?" Poppy pointed, "Look darling, that coach over there, perhaps it's going to Sorrento."

They walked down the hill and spoke to the driver. "Sorrento?" asked Russ. "Si, we go Nizza 'otel." There was room so he agreed to take them. Once aboard and on their way the couple wondered how far the Nizza was from the Carlton.

It was late afternoon when they arrived, Poppy went into the hotel to ask directions to the Carlton while Russ waited outside to check for a taxi in case they needed one. As he stood on the kerb a white van pulled up in front of him the door slid open, and he was dragged inside. The van then drove off.

Poppy came out of the hotel and looked around for Russ. She couldn't phone him as they had only brought one mobile. She started to panic, then took several deep breathes. Now calmer she decided what to do.

Finding her way back to the Carlton she went up their room and got Russ's passport then went to the local Police Station.

The white van parked up on the drive of a rented villa situated miles from anywhere. Two men dragged Russ inside and tied him to a chair. One of the men spoke, "Now Harry, this is what is going to happen." Russ spoke over him, "I am not Harry, my name is Russ Parsons, I'm a schoolteacher from Slough, you've got the wrong man." He was shown a photo. "It looks like me but it's not me," shouted Russ. The man told him they had visited the Nizza hotel, saying they were friends of Bullen, and were told you were on a coach trip and what time you would be back. We waited. Then you arrived and stepped out of the coach outside the Nizza Hotel. Russ bowed his head; he didn't speak all he could think about was Poppy. The man continued speaking. "We will stay her tonight then back to the UK tomorrow when Mr Bloom's private jet arrives.

The NCA arrived at the Nizza Hotel in the morning and waited. When they saw Bullen enter the coach, they followed it. On reaching Positano Bullen went for a walk around then sat at an outside table of a small café, he ordered a beer. The two Officers then sat at the same table. "The game's up Harry, you know that don't you?" He looked frightened. "Did Marcus send you?" "No, mate, but he knows you're in Sorrento staying at the Nizza hotel, we're from the NCA, that's Ethan I'm Finn." The other officer nodded. "Nothing worse than a bent copper, eh Finn?" said Ethan. Finn agreed. " So, you must come with us back to London today," said Finn. "Got a warrant, foreign country and all?" Bullen asked cockily. "No, mate we don't, but hey, we'll just leave you to the boys Marcus sent." Harry looked around anxiously. Ethan spoke, "we hear you owe him 2 million quid, you're a dead man, unless you got the cash, have you?" Harry shook his head. "Come on Ethan let's go." Harry stood up, "no wait, I 'll come with you."

The three men arrived at the hotel and went up to Harry's room. He packed his bag and gave the officers his passport. They all left for the airport.

Rory Telford was in his office when the call came through from the officers in Italy. He was told they had Bullen and would be back in England later that day. Yes, this case was a total success, he thought. He went into the rest room to make a coffee, the tv was on, he looked up when the news came on, it featured a report of a missing holidaymaker named Russ Parsons from England. He was last seen outside a hotel in Sorrento Italy. A picture of Russ was then shown. Rory couldn't believe it. He guessed instantly that he was a Bullen lookalike and had been abducted by Bloom's men, this poor guy is in real danger, he thought. Assuming the men would probably arrive in London some time tomorrow, he sent a task force to stake out the restaurant.

He was right, at 11am the following day a car parked up outside the Oxford and three men got out, one was Russ Parsons. The two men were taken into custody and Russ was taken to hospital. Three officers entered the restaurant and arrested Bloom.

On advice from the police, Poppy had returned home to wait for news. When she heard that Russ was safe, she rushed to the hospital. He had suffered cuts and bruises but otherwise was in good health.

They hugged and kissed then shared what information they each had about what had gone on. "Do you know, Poppy, one police officer told me I was just in the wrong place at the wrong time, do you know what I thought?" "No darling, tell me." Russ smiled, "he should have said wrong face at the wrong time."

WORSLEY MANOR

Worsley Manor was built in 1850 for Sir Josiah Williams a cotton mill owner in Birlam, Wiltshire. He was married with one son called Samuel. Josiah was a good man who cared for his workers and paid them well. He died in 1880. Samuel inherited the house and the business. He was not a good man, he was a gambler a womaniser and cruel to his wife and two daughters, they hated him and eventually moved into a cottage on the estate. He died a bankrupt in 1913. In 1914 his wife accepted a government offer to turn Worsley Manor into a hospital during the war for sick and wounded soldiers. Later the family moved away, and the Manor was bought by an Educational Trust and became a school. By 1960 the Manor was empty and falling into disrepair.

Ivor Clements bought the Manor as a retirement home in 2000. He had made his fortune in the gold and diamond trade. The property was repaired and renovated a swimming pool and tennis court were built within the 50-acre estate.

It was late December and the Clements family had gathered to spend a week together at Christmastime at the Manor. There was the two daughters, Megan and Miriam, their husbands, Lewis, and Craig plus the three grandchildren, Jessica 12, Grace 10, and Zac aged 7.

Over lunch in the dining room one day, they were discussing what to do in the afternoon. It was decided the adults would visit the newly built stables and the children would explore the woods. Everyone wrapped up warmly as the weather although dry was very cold. As the children approached the Japanese bridge that spanned the lake, they saw a woman standing halfway across looking into the water. "Hello, who are you?" asked Jessica. "Beg your pardon miss, I'm Molly."

Looking at her clothes, Gracie asked, "Do you work in the kitchen?" "Yes Miss I do". Grace looked worried, "perhaps you should go back, it's very cold and you're not wearing a coat." "Yes miss, I will.". Molly turned and set off towards the Manor. The children stood watching as she walked into a clump of tall bushes but never came out the other side. They were puzzled and ran to search the bushes, but no Molly. Now bored they went back over the bridge and into the woods.

In the evening, after dinner, the family sat down to watch 'It's a Wonderful Life', then later Megan packed Grace and Zac off to bed. While tucking them in Zac said they had met a lady called Molly, "Was she an old lady?" "No said Grace, I think she works in the kitchen." "She must have been cold, piped up Zac, she didn't have a coat on." She kissed them both goodnight. She went downstairs and told the others of her conversation with the children. "Just their imagination", said Lewis. "No, said Jessica indignantly, it's true, I was there." "OK Jessie, we believe you said Miriam, now pop along to bed, there's a good girl." Jessica went to bed in the room she shared with the other two.

At around 2am a loud shriek could be heard, a single note high pitched then stopped suddenly. The children woke up, they felt a cold wind in the room which made the curtains shake. Then the voice of Molly could be heard, whispering, "I'm sorry, I'm not alone." Then silence and everything went back to normal. The three children stared at each other, "say nothing to the others, we'll keep this to ourselves," said Jessica. They nodded in agreement.

"You're very quiet this morning," said Megan over breakfast. "Did you children hear anything last night?" They looked up from their cereal bowls, "no mummy answered Grace, did you?" Flustered, "No of course not," replied Megan. After breakfast the children decided to explore the house, they went to the kitchen first. Mrs Molloy the cook was chopping vegetables when they entered, she stopped, "and what can I do for you little'uns?"

"Where's Molly?" asked Zac. "No Molly here my love, just me." "Are you sure," said Jessica as she looked in the larder. "Of course, I'm sure now be off with you I've got work to do." As they closed the kitchen door Grace noticed a small staircase, "what's up here do you think?" Jessica looked, "let's have a look, probably led the servant's bedrooms in the olden days," she suggested. At the top was a narrow carpet less corridor with rooms off. "Hold my hand Jessie, I'm scared," said Zac. She did as they entered the first room, it was empty except for an iron single bed. They sat on it then a voice behind them said "hello." Looking round they saw Molly. "This was my room until something….," her voice trailed away. "Something happened?" asked Jessica. Ignoring her Molly asked if she could talk to them again because it made her happy. Of course you can they all said together. She then disappeared. That night, again around 2am, there came a crashing banging noise, Ivor awoke and turning to his wife Evie, said "I'll go and check." As he left the bedroom he ran into Craig and Lewis on the landing, "Sounds like it's coming from the wine cellar, let's go chaps." On entering the winery, the devastation was vast, wine racks had been pulled down and broken bottles covered the floor then from a darkened recess a glow appeared a tall thin man could be seen with staring eyes, long hair, and dressed in Edwardian clothes. The figure then pointed at Ivor, "this is my house it is not your house, begone." With that the spectre disappeared leaving the recess in darkness again. The three men stood in silence then Ivor spoke, "scotch anyone?" The others nodded. As Ivor was pouring the drinks the loud shriek could be heard once again.

The following morning Miriam and Megan drove into town to do a bit of shopping they visited various shops ending up at a small museum. Upon entering they were greeted by Foster Wilks the elderly Curator, "hello ladies can I help you?"

They asked him if there was any information on Worsley Manor, "of course, he replied, follow me." He led them into a room which among other things contained the history of Birlam. On one wall were two paintings, one of a Victorian gentleman underneath was written Sir Josiah Williams the other was Samuel Williams, son of Josiah. Both paintings were acquired by the museum in a content's sale in 1960. On a table were some other items from the Manor also a slim paperback titled 'The History of Worsley Manor' written by a local author. Miriam bought the book, thanked Mr Wilks for his help and they left the museum in search of lunch.

That evening over drinks the whole family discussed recent events, by now they all had read the book. Megan spoke first, "well, the house is obviously haunted, would you agree?" They all nodded. "But why is there no mention of hauntings before?" asked Ivor. "Well, the way I see it, said Megan, is that since the Williams, no other family have lived here, you Ivor and Evie are the first." Then Craig spoke, "so the children were right about Molly, as the book states she was a kitchen maid raped by Samuel , when she realised she was pregnant asked him for help he sacked her saying we don't want a maid with child working here. She left the Manor and threw herself off the bridge into the lake where she drowned." Miriam had listened to everyone, "I can't stay here with Jessica, then turning to Lewis, we must leave, darling. it's not safe." "We can't leave, my love, tomorrow is Christmas day." They then discussed a plan of action.

That night, after the children were in bed, they all gathered in the large foyer and stood beneath the chandelier as they faced the grand staircase. Calling out in one voice they shouted – we will never leave this house. Silence, then there he was, walking down the stairs in a rage, "you WILL leave my house, or you all will die." Stalemate. Nobody moved, nobody spoke. Then it happened. Molly walked down the stairs, her arms above her head and between her hands she held an antique sword, with just one step above Samuel she shouted, "No, you must die," with that she plunged the sword into his back then let go and stepped back. In an instant he disappeared only the sword could be seen as it slid silently down the staircase. Molly then called out, "forgive me." They answered her, "we do." She spoke again, "I love you; I love your children, I will always be here if you will let me." Ivor spoke, "we are your friends Molly, please stay." "Thank you, thank you so much." She waved at them then disappeared. "Wow, said Craig, well that's one Christmas eve no one will believe."

Christmas day went very well, eating drinking, present opening, what more could you ask. And just behind the Xmas tree stood the waif thin Molly happy at last with a family that she was so cruelly denied in real life.

⚬⟨⟩⟩⟩⚬

SPACEMAN – A FANTASY TALE

It was a small island just off the Devonshire coast, a few properties were dotted about also the odd farm or two with sheep or cows, but mostly there were green fields and a lake. 10-year-old Marty was sat on a fallen tree poking the ground with a stick, he was bored. He then heard what sounded like an engine noise, it grew louder but looking around he couldn't see anything. Feeling scared he hid behind the tree. A spaceship then appeared it was shaped like an arrowhead. A man exited and pointed some sort of remote-control box, the airship disappeared. The man looked lost, so Marty approached him, the man turned, "who are you?" "I'm Marty Barty," "Barty Tarty?" "No, not Barty Tarty it's Marty Barty, anyway what's your name?" "I'm Buck T Banner space traveller and hill climber at your service but you can call me Buck." Marty smiled, "glad to meet you Buck and welcome." Buck looked around, "where am I?" "You're lost," said Marty. "I know I am, so where is this place?" "I've already told you." Buck then noticed a fallen road sign, picking it up he read out loud 'Welcome to Yerlost. Marty cut in, "that's what I said." Throwing down the sign he asked, "This IS Earth though, isn't it?" "Of course it is, replied Marty, where have you been?" Buck rubbed his eyes, "I've been out on my TM." "Tiny mind?" suggested Marty. "No stupid, Time Machine, he softened, I'm sorry." Marty's eyes widened, "can I see it?" Buck held up the remote box, "afraid not I've switched it to INMO – Invisible Mode, so it can't be stolen, God I'm starving." Marty rummaged in his backpack, "how about a sandwich and a Jaffa cake?" "Smashing, that would be great." They both sat down on the fallen tree.

"Now Marty tell me all about yourself." "I'm an orphan." "Yes, what else?" Marty looked at him, "an orphan, sir." "No, no not sir, where do you live?" Marty pointed, "about a mile that way, it's a big building with lots of bedrooms, we call it the....Buck butted in "orphanage", no the House, eight children and me live there." "Who looks after you?" "O, Auntie and Uncle look here he comes now." Marty stood up and shouted, "Hi shaky, over here, he then turned to Buck, you might find him a bit odd." The man approached them, "how do I find thee young Marty, well I trust?" "Yes, very well Uncle." "Now who be this, a stranger me thinks, if I'm not mistaken." (The boy wasn't lying Buck thought to himself). "A Spaceman, Uncle, with a time machine." He stepped forward, "Buck T Banner sir, or Buck for short." "Welcome young man, you have the honour of addressing Shakespeare Bronte, my parents were of a literary persuasion." Buck shook his hand, "you're Shaky?" "No, perfectly healthy, thank you for asking, now if you have nowhere to stay, Mrs Bellows has a B&B, if you are interested." "That sounds perfect, lead the way." As they walked away the remote box fell to the floor, unseen.

Not far from the fallen tree stood two large oil drums, asleep inside were two teenagers, 17-year-old Jigger and Rascal aged 16, they were members of a gang called the meanie-mouths. Jigger stood up rubbing his eyes, "hey Rascal, I've just had the weirdest dream, there was this spaceman with a time machine." "So did I Jigger, we must have had the same dream, spooky eh?" Jigger yawned and scratched his head, "Have you got any of the food left we nicked from that farmhouse window?" Rascal took something out of his pocket, "there's a bit of pizza left." "Pizza, ha, I remember the days when there used to be a meat pie or apple tarts cooling slowly beside an open kitchen window, but now pizza, REALLY!" "Aw, give it a rest Jigger." "Less of your cheek young Rascal, what shall we do?" Rascal thought for a moment, "we could get the rest of the gang and beat up the kids from the orphanage." "No, I'm fed up doing that, anyway they always win." Jigger suggested playing football with Marty. "Play with him, you must be joking." "No, said Jigger, I mean he could be the football," they both laughed. "You're a rascal, Rascal, and no mistake."

As they were walking, Rascal kicked something he bent down and picked it up, "it's some sort of control box." As he fiddled with it the time machine engine started up, he threw it on the ground, they both screamed. Jigger then picked up the remote box, "I know what this is, he pushed some of the buttons and the engine stopped, that was no dream we had." Rascal looked at the box, "that's not a million pounds." Jigger sighed, "not that dream dopey, there's a time machine somewhere round here and this controls it." "Not much good if we can't see it." Jigger smiled to himself, "we will once we've had a word with Marty, come on let's find him."

Buck and Shaky arrived at the B&B, Marty had decided to return home. Mrs Bellows signed Buck in then he and Shaky entered the sitting room. "Now Buck tell me your story." He cleared his throat then began. " Eight years ago, I was a happily married to Donna, we had two children, the twins Paul and Paula, they were 6 years old. We all lived together in a little house at Athos on the planet Bounty. I had recently discovered the mountain Rexo and walked up and down it 6 times to make it my own, that's the law on Bounty. Well one day we decided to have a picnic at a lovely place called Twix Island, along the Milky Way just before you reach Mars. After eating our sandwiches, we were just about to have our pudding which Donna had made – she called it our planet sweet. Anyway, my phone rang, it was the Hill society – the Honourable Institute of Land Lubbers – some people were stuck up Mount Portus, I had to rescue them. I found them and led them to safety. When I returned to Twix Island it had gone." "Do you mean disappeared," asked Shaky. " Sort of, continued Buck, it had floated away, it happens sometimes, in space. So, I have spent the last 8 years searching for my family. I've discovered some mountains in that time, I can tell you. I have been back and forward in time but without success. One day I'll find them, I know I will. So that is my story." Shaky was quite moved, "well, well, a sad story indeed."

Changing the subject and attempting to cheer Buck up Shaky asked him if he would like to come to the village hall the following day at 2pm. The orphanage is putting on a show to raise money for charity, all the children are doing a turn he added. Buck said he'd love to.

As Marty was walking home, he bumped into Jigger and Rascal. "Hallo frog face, said Jigger, lost sommat 'ave ya?" Marty sighed, "get out of my way meanie-mouth." "You're a bright chap, must hear all the gossip round here, we were wondering if you'd seen any strangers lately." "Yea, with a Time Machine," added Rascal. "You've found the remcon box, haven't you? "said Marty. "No, we haven't, said Jigger quickly, what's a remcon box?" "No idea." Jigger produced the box and waved it above his head, "so what's this then?" Marty made a grab for the box but missed. "Tell me how it works and I'll give it back to you." "No deal Jigger," replied Marty as he walked off.

The following morning he went to the B&B and spoke to Buck telling him about the remote-control box. Together they went to the field, standing by the oil drums Buck shouted, "anybody in there?" " There's no one here," replied Jigger. "Give me the box," "only if you show me the spaceship." "It's a deal." Jigger stood up and gave the box to Buck who then pressed the code word and the spaceship appeared. "Can I go inside?" "No, now clear off before I active the 'shrink' button and you will be 3 foot tall." Jigger screamed and ran off. Buck and Marty then headed for the village hall. Out of the blue Marty suddenly said, I wish you were my dad.

On reaching the hall Marty went backstage as Buck went to the front row and sat a chair marked 'reserved'. The house lights went down as the stage lit up. Shaky stepped forward and thanked all the people for coming, "I'll start the show with a speech from King Lear," the audience groaned. When he finished the audience clapped, "would you like to hear some more?" Silence. "I'm only joking, now put your hands together for Lily singing 'Over the Rainbow'.

After the third act had finished, Marty entered and walked to the front of the stage. "This is a poem I wrote, it's called 'I Wish'."

> I wish that I could swim, I wish I could swim
> I wish that I could spree like the fishes in the sea
> But I only have dreams for fins, yes only have dreams for fins
>
> I wish that I could fly, I wish I could fly
> I wish I could soar like the birds up in the sky
> But I only have dreams for wings, yes only have dreams for wings
>
> I wish I had a dad; I really wish I had a dad
> I wish I had a mum and then I'd not be sad
> But I only have dreams of love, only dreams of love.

Marty bowed saying thank you for listening and left the stage to tremendous applause. Then Shaky entered, "the final act this afternoon is a bit of fun written and presented by Billie and Bob." From either side of the stage came a boy and a girl, they turned to face each other then Bob said to Billie, "Now listen to me."

I don't drink – I don't smoke – I don't swear.

Billie: If that's the truth you can cut off my hair.

Bob: I don't cheat – I don't steal – I don't lie.

Billie: You gotta be kidding, that's pie in the sky – NOT TRUE.

Bob: Says you. Billie: That's true.

Bob: Aw, poo! Never ever had a drink in my life – never smoked a pipe- couldn't swear to save my life.

Billie: NOT TRUE. Bob: Says you. Billie: That's true.

Bob: Aw, poo! I've never cheated on a friend or a pal – never stolen anything – never lied to me gal.

Billie: Your GAL? Bob: If I had one. Billie: None of its true.

Bob: Says you. Billie: That's true.

Bob: Aw, poo! What about you?

Billie: Me? Well, I've never touched sherry beer whisky or wine, never smoked a cigarette and my language is fine. Never had a reason to cheat on anyone, never stolen anything and lying's just not done.

Bob: NOT TRUE.

Billie: I'm just the perfect one. Bob: NOT TRUE.

Billie: So much nicer that you, my chum. Bob: NOT TRUE.

Billie: We could go on like this till I'm 102.

Bob: That's true. Billie: Says thee – I agree.

Bob: Shall we? (They link arms).

Together: We've never had a drink, or smoked a pipe, never swore or cheated on a pal, never stolen anything, or lied to a gal.

(They both stop and take a deep breath – then continue).

Never touched sherry beer whisky or wine, never smoked a cigarette and out language is fine. Never had a reason to cheat on anyone, never stolen anything and lying just not done.

(They stop – look at the audience – then at each other).

Bob: Who are we kidding? Billie: None of this is true.

Bob: What a load of rubbish. Billie: I agree with you.

Together: NOT TRUE. (They link arms and leave the stage).

The audience stand up cheering and clapping except for Buck, he remained seated with tears rolling down his cheeks and repeating the words Paul and Paula. Shaky and the cast return to the stage. "Let's hear it one more time for the children." the audience applaud. He thanks everyone for coming and the people leave.

Shaky sat down beside Buck and placed a hand on his shoulder, "me thinks I know what ails you my friend, Bob and Billie are your missing children are they not?" Buck nods. "In that case I may have another shock for you." He stood up and facing the stage called out Auntie, Auntie, are you there? Donna walked forward she stopped and stared, "what the….Buck, is that you?" She jumped down from the stage and they both hugged each other tightly. Donna spoke, " the island moved away so fast and being strangers we three lost our memories, Shaky found us and has been looking after us these past 8 years. The minute I saw you all the past memories came back. Let me call the children." She went through a door beside the stage and after a few minutes returned with the children. "I knew we had a daddy." shouted Paula, then more hugging ensued. "But we don't remember our real names," said Donna. Buck pointed to each one in turn, Paul, Paula, and Donna. " Of course, said Donna, I remember now," the other two nodded, Shaky, who had remained silent during the reunion, asked them all to sit down. When you told me your sad story Buck, he began, the puzzle started to come together. He had spent the morning at the islands Historical Records Office. 8 years ago, Yerlost was called Twix Island, when the new Mayor was appointed, he changed the name to Yerlost, that was a mayors prerogative, still is. He thought the sudden swift movement through space of the island had caused the Banner family to lose their memory.

If you have lived on the island for some time, sudden movements don't affect you.

He found the family wandering around so took them in and gave them new names. Buck jumped up, "Shaky you are our hero, we will never forget you." "I'm no hero, Buck, but thank you." He then invited Buck to stay at the orphanage overnight.

After breakfast the Banners were getting ready to leave and return home. But there was one more thing Buck wanted to do, first he had a quiet word with Shaky then with his family. Marty was still sitting at the table when Buck approached him and sat down. "Tell me Marty would you like to come with us and be a part of our family?" The boy burst into tears and threw himself at Buck, "yes," was his answer. Buck turned to the others, "say hello to Marty Banner, your new Brother." Welcome to the family Marty they replied. "Off you go my boy and pack a suitcase, said Buck, the spaceship takes off in 1 hour."

❖

THE UNHAPPY KING

A story told for one and all to adults big and children small

To be alive in the 1400's meant one of two things, to be rich and happy or poor and sad. Simplistically put I know, but with this tale there is an anomaly. A rich king who is sad and a poor jester who is happy. Let us visit the town of Onslovia, located in Europe. Here lived King Peter. On this particular morning he was in the Throne Room as usual when in walked Olaf, the Captain of his army. Let us listen in to their conversation.

Olaf: "Good morning your Majesty".

King: "Good morning captain".

Olaf: "The army is on parade awaiting your inspection, Sire".

King: "Very well, I'll come" (he *answered tiredly).*

Olaf: "Beggin' your pardon Sire, you are not very happy these days, are you?"

King: "No captain I am not".

Olaf: "If I may be so bold as to ask why?"

King: "I am not happy because the Queen is unhappy".

Olaf: "Ah, right Sire, I see, ah, if I might boldly ask why?"

King: "The Queen is not happy because the Princess is not happy", he answered crossly.

Olaf: "Right Sire, all clear now, (he paused) err. beggin' your pardon just one tiny time again Sire, if you please".

King: "Get on with it man".

Olaf: "Well your Highness, why is the Princess unhappy?"

King: "For goodness sake, the Princess is unhappy because the people of Onslovia are unhappy".

Olaf: "Gotcha Sire, gotcha (a long pause) just let me get this straight, please don't hit me, you are unhappy because the Queen, the Princess and the people are unhappy, am I right?"

King: "Yes captain you are perfectly right. Have you finished talking now?"

Olaf: "Well, just one more tiny little question – why all the sadness?"

King: "I DO NOT KNOW. Can I inspect the army now?"

Olaf: "Most certainly Sire (he bowed) after you Sire".

Later that day, Captain Olaf was again in the Throne Room when in walked Patches, the Court jester. Let's listen in.

Olaf: "Hello Patches me lad! Tell me, what is your job around here, what do you do?"

Patches: "Well, I keep the Royal Family amused".

Olaf: "How do you do that then?"

Patches: "With a funny joke, a pretty dance or a merry song".

Olaf: "Well, it ain't working, is it my lad?"

Patches: "No Captain it ain't, I mean it isn't".

Olaf: "Perhaps you're not funny anymore, perhaps we should give you the sack?"

Patches: "Oh no, don't do that".

Olaf: "Tell ME a joke then and I'll see if you are still funny".

Patches: "Alright then. A man went to the doctor, he said I've got a head like a turnip, three ears, two noses and a mouth the wrong way around, what am I? The doctor said, ugly".

Olaf: "Very funny, you can keep your job – for now. But if I was you, I'd find out why the people are unhappy".

Patches: "Who should I ask?"

Olaf: The wisest man around here must be Ali Ben Sage, he's from the East you know".

Patches: "What, you mean Southend?"

Olaf: "No you fool, the Far East".

Patches: "Where does he live?"

Olaf: "Try asking Woo-Woo the wise owl".

Patches: "Where does Woo-Woo live?"

Olaf: "You're not very bright for a jester, are you? Try the Rhyming Forest, that's the one you want. Now be off with you".

So, Patches set off for the forest, he took with him a basket containing sandwiches and a flask of water. After walking a very long way he finally reached the Rhyming Forest. A bat flew over his head and gave him a fright.

Patches: "That made me jump said Patches, I wish I wasn't so alone".

Bobo: Hello young sir what's your name, I'm Bobo the monkey will you play a game?"

Patches: "I'm Patches, pleased to meet you (No answer). Why doesn't he speak? of course I have to rhyme. My name is Patches to meet you I'm pleased – atishoo – forgive me, I think I just sneezed".

Bobo: "Bless you dear Patches, you funny boy, what's in the basket a game or a toy?"

Patches: "No sorry just my sandwiches. I think I'd better be off now".

And with that he walked further into the forest. Suddenly, he heard a loud squawking above him, it was a bird.

Polly: "My name is Polly and I say to you what is your name and how do you do?"

Patches: "My name is Patches to see you I'm pleased – atishoo – excuse me, I think I just sneezed".

Polly: "Patches my dear come closer come near, how can I help you what do you want here?"

He then asked Polly where Woo-woo lived. Polly showed him the right road to take, wished him luck then flew off. After walking a bit further, he came to a clearing and decided to eat. Reaching for his sandwiches Patches heard a noise in the nearby bushes.

Woo: "To-woo, to-woo, who are you?"

Patches: "I'm called Patches, how do you do?"

Woo: "My name is Woo-Woo, who do you seek? Be quick with your answer try not to squeak".

Patches: "It's you I seek; I'm not a mouse and I never squeak".

Woo: "What a pity, I just fancied a mouse".

He told the owl all about the unhappy King and asked where he could find Ali Ben Sage.

Woo: "The man you seek lives in a cave, go and visit if you're brave".

Patches: "Where is the cave – I'm very brave?"

Woo: "Your quest dear boy is now at an end, the man you seek lives just round the bend. To-woo to-woo, goodbye to you".

Patches followed the path round the bend, as it became straight there in front of him was a large boulder blocking his way. Well, he thought I wasn't expecting this, I'll give it a good push. It didn't move. As he went to push it again there was a puff of smoke, the boulder disappeared and there stood Ali Ben Sage.

Ali: "Who calls me?"

Patches: "Here we go again, my name is Patches to see you…

Ali: "Let me stop you there, I understand everyone, and everyone understands me".

Patches then explained to Ali the unhappiness in Onslovia. The wise man listened carefully, he agreed to go with Patches back to Onslovia. Meanwhile, back at the Palace, Princess Mary was talking to the King.

Mary: "Oh father what am I to do?"

King: "Whatever is the matter dear child?"

Mary: "I am in love with Prince Rupert of Farnhamia and he is in love with me, but he won't marry me".

King: "Why ever not?"

Mary: "He says that Onslovia is ugly, and the people are always sad and unhappy".

King: "Have no fear my daughter for I believe that Patches, our loyal Court Jester has gone in search of an answer to our problems".

Just as the King was speaking, Patches and Ali arrived at the Palace gates. The King went to meet them and returned with Ali.

Ali: "So, your Majesty there is much unhappiness in the kingdom of Onslovia, is that correct?"

King: "Yes O wise one, that is true".

Ali: "Let us go then to the highest tower of the Palace and look down over Onslovia".

This is what the two men did. Looking down over the Kingdom Ali was the first to speak.

Ali: "Now tell me Sire, are the people well fed?"

King: "Yes, they are. See all the remnants of uneaten food".

Ali: "Yes, I see. Have the people enough to drink?"

King: "Why yes, see all the empty flagons and bottles".

Ali: "Yes, I see. Tell me do the flowers bloom brightly and the trees grow strong and bushy?"

King: "Well now you come to mention it, no they do not".

Ali: "Down there is the cause of all your problems".

King: "I do not understand wise one".

Ali: "Litter Sire, so much litter everywhere. On the paths, the fields, and the gardens of the people. It makes Onslovia look ugly and the people unhappy".

King: "Well I never, you are absolutely right. But what do I do?"

Ali: "You must place litter-containers or bins, for short, throughout the Kingdom. Then instruct the people on how to use them. A clean Onslovia will become a happy Kingdom for all".

And this is what the King did. The people started to take a pride in their villages. Soon everyone was happy again. Do you want to know something else? Prince Rupert did marry the Princess. You know what I'm going to say next, don't you? They all lived happily ever after.

LIFE AND DEATH

The first time I kissed my father was in his open coffin at the funeral wake. I may have before as a very young boy, but I don't remember. The last time I hugged him was at my mother's funeral when I was 10 years old. My older brother and sister shared many family intimacies with him, I think he just didn't have any room left in his heart for me.

I never thought, sitting here in my study, that writing an autobiography would stir up so many past forgotten memories I find it odd how so many sad moments leap to mind more than happy ones. I recall the day I left home aged 17 to live in a bedsit, my siblings still lived at home, I hugged them both then turned to my father, he just shook my hand. Anyway, this all getting a bit maudlin, I'm not a bitter old man, I mean 60 these days isn't old, I'm actually a very happy chappy!

I decided to write down things as they come to mind then later put them in chronological order. So, my brother Patrick is 48 and married to Rita they have two children and live in America. He is a science teacher. My sister Anna aged 52 - back in the day she would have been called a spinster - a horrible word, I think of her as a free spirit, anyway, she worked as a Senior Nurse until she developed a heart condition which forced her to retire early. She lives in Roseleaf Cottage.

When I was 20, I joined the Army and served for 25 happy years with the Royal Marines. I now work as a civil servant with the Parole Board.

Anna knocked on the study door and entered, she went over to the desk, "Still writing your memoirs are you, Martin? she said with a smile, dinner's ready." "OK my love, I'll be right down," Martin replied as he closed the laptop.

Two days later he returned to his study and continued with the biography.

I was married for 12 years until my wife left me for her lover. We later divorced. Around this time Anna's condition got worse so I sold my house and moved into the cottage so I could take care of her.

Martin continued writing. Some three days later Martin and Anna visited the Redgrave Theatre in Farnham to watch a play.

When they returned home, they found the house had been burgled. The robber took everything of value including Anna's jewellery, she was so upset as most of it had been given to her by our mother. To make matters worse, the next day she fell for an online scam, they emptied her bank account. When Martin contacted the insurance company about the robbery they refused to pay out as the 'Direct Debit' had not been paid. When he told them about the scam, they still refused to pay even though Anna had been with them for years.

When Anna became depressed about these latest events, Martin tried to comfort her he told not to worry about money as he still had plenty in the bank after selling his house.

The last straw came for Anna was when she was out shopping, looking in a pawnbroker's window she saw some of her jewellery, she went inside and spoke to the owner. He denied any of the items were stolen and told her to go away. When she said she would go to the police he threatened her. She went home swallowed all her prescription pills and lay down on the sofa.

When Martin came home from work and found her, he immediately called for an ambulance, there was a note on the coffee table, it read, I'm sorry Martin I just can't go on. He was heartbroken, then his sadness turned to anger, I must do something he thought, criminals must not go unpunished. He decided then and there what he would do.

After a late lunch Oliver Carr returned to his office at Bardon & Sykes Insurance Agents. As he entered, a tall, bearded man wearing glasses stood up, "I have been waiting for you". "Really said Oliver, as he sat down, how can I help?" The stranger remained standing, "I have something for you". "What might that be", said Oliver uneasily. The man placed his briefcase on the desk and opened it, "Justice", he replied as he removed the Glock 23 pistol with silencer attached. He shot Oliver through the heart then replaced the gun in the briefcase and closed it. He left the building.

It was around 6pm and getting dark as the pawnshop owner, Dev Amir, approached the door to lock up for the day, suddenly, a stranger pushed the door open and entered the shop. "I'm sorry Mr Amir for the late hour but I've got something to show you". Dev sighed, "OK, but make it quick". The man placed his briefcase on the counter and opened it and removed the gun. "No, no, I don't deal in weapons", said Dev. "I didn't come here to sell it I came to shoot you". Dev turned to run but the bullet hit him in the back of his head, he fell to the floor.

The stranger dragged the body behind the counter out of sight. He then replaced the weapon in the briefcase removed the keys from the door and left the shop locking the door behind him. On his way back to his car he threw the keys into a nearby waste bin.

The car parked opposite number 27 Conway Street had been there since early morning. Around 9am a man left the house and headed off up the street. 30 minutes later the driver of the car crossed the street and went round the back of number 27 and entered the house.

At 11.30am the occupier returned to the house and let himself in, he placed the bag he was carrying onto the kitchen worktop and began to unpack it.

The stranger approached silently, gun in hand. "Your name is Cole Preston, a common thief". Cole looked up, "You'll have to prove it, the police can't", he replied, cockily. "I don't have to prove anything, I KNOW you are a low-life thief", he then raised the gun and shot Cole through the heart. The stranger of course was Martin.

After leaving 27 Conway Street Martin returned home and went to his study. His next visit was to write about his childhood but instead he wrote about the murders. He explained how he contacted one of his old army buddies who put him in touch with a man who sold him a gun. Then through his job was able to open private files and documents until he found Cole Preston.

The CID team at Redland Police Station was a hive of activity. The evidence proved that the same gun was used in all three murders. DCI Arnott was convinced it was the work of a professional hitman. But what he couldn't figure out was why a gang boss would pay top dollar to kill an insurance salesman, a pawnbroker, and a small-time thief. "What do you think, Chiv?", he asked DS Chivers. "It seems personal, a sort of revenge thing", he replied. "Yes, Arnott continued, but what's the connection?"

After 'due diligence' as they say, a suspect was in the frame but proving it was tricky. The team went back through all the evidence, CCTV, witnesses' statements, victims' financials, their histories, and their families' histories. The evidence grew stronger. A single name finally emerged, Martin Newton.

At 6am the following morning armed police moved quietly along Milton Lane, following behind were DCI Arnott and DS Chivers. They reached Roseleaf Cottage and forced open the door and went in shouting 'Police'. After the call of 'all clear' the two Detectives then went in, the senior armed police officer tapped Arnott on the shoulder, "You best go upstairs Sir, look in the study".

Jim Arnott stood in the doorway and stared at the body on the chair by the desk. He moved closer and saw the Glock 23 gun lying on the floor and the bullet hole in Newton's head. Coming closer he saw the closed laptop with a post-it note on top.

DS Chivers entered the study "That must be Martin Newton guv, our assassin". Jim turned and looked at the DS, "Yes Chiv, the beard and glasses were obviously a disguise, but here's the thing, why would a hired hitman with three kills in 7 days be living in a two-bed cottage with roses round the door and then decide to commit suicide?"

"I guess we'll never know guv." "Oh yes, I think we will Chiv," he said as he lifted the note from the laptop on which was written the words, password for computer – Life&Death.

THE LETTER

I love the smell of a library thought Alfie. The books and wood polish had a calming effect on him as he sat at a table in the book lined room of the university library working on an essay on the writings of 14th century monks. He looked up as his roommate, Leon, sat down opposite him, "How's it going Al?" he whispered. "Oh, so-so, what I need now is a book on Latin translation." He left the table and wandered along the tall bookcases. He found what he was looking for and returned to the table. "You appear to be successful dear boy," said Leon. "Yes," he replied as he flicked through the pages, he stopped suddenly as he noticed a folded piece of paper between the pages toward the back of the book. He removed it assuming it was a bookmark from a previous reader. But no, it was a letter. "Look at this Leon," he said as he handed it to him. "What have we here, a love letter perhaps or a suicide note?" He read it aloud but quietly.

Meet me at starfish 4. at midnight.

Bring a spade. Noli esse sero.

From Gustav.

"All a bit mysterious, what's the Latin in English?" he said as he handed it back. Alfie stared at the letter, "It's certainly interesting, a mystery worth looking into, but perhaps for some other day. The phrase in English is 'do not be late' He refolded it and placed it in his shoulder bag. Now back to the monks."

Alfie and Leon had shared a room at Portsmouth University for the past year, he was studying History and Leon was studying Law. They started at the same time and became firm friends. Of the two, Leon was the more outgoing he loved drinking and partying. Alfie was a trifle more serious although he did enjoy going to the Uni bar for a drink and good conversation.

On the Friday Alfie was on his way home for the weekend as his sister Glenda was getting married the following day. He was to walk her down the aisle instead of their father as he had died of cancer two years previously. Alfie had only met Kenny Gordon, Glenda's fiance, a couple of times but he seemed a nice enough chap. He was older than her and owned a successful antique shop.

As the train pulled into Midhurst station, Alfie waved to his mum and Glenda waiting on the platform. After hugs all round it was then into the car as mum drove to the house.

They sat in the lounge chatting and catching up with each other's news. Glenda, who was sitting beside Alfie then turned to him saying "So, what has my little historian brother bought me for a wedding gift I wonder?" "What?" he replied in mock horror, "I'm a schoolboy with no income living on a student loan." "Of course, I'm only joking, she said, you big lummox." she said laughingly. She paused for a moment then became serious, "Just you being at my wedding is enough for me Alfie, thank you." To lighten the mood, he placed his hands on Glenda's shoulders and looked into her eyes, "Is it alright if I wear my college T-Shirt and shorts?" His answer came when a sofa cushion hit him on the head.

The wedding went off without a problem and come Sunday afternoon Alfie was on the train back to Portsmouth. His thoughts went back to the library and that letter. He remembered, as a child, walking bare foot on Pagham beach and finding a starfish lying there or a fish with five legs as he childishly called it. His reverie suddenly ended, of course that's it, he thought, 1. 2. 3. 4. 5. starfish 4. that's the answer, but damn-it what does it mean.

Leon and Alfie were in their room one lunchtime. Alfie was re-reading the letter he then handed it to his friend saying, "With your astute legal mind what does it tell you?" Leon took it and held it up to the light, "Ah, a rose motif watermark a paper of quality." He then read the note several times, he handed it back saying, "Well, my not so learned friend, this is what I deduce, 1. Fine quality paper. 2. The text was written using a fountain pen – probably a Parker. The use of Latin denotes the author to be intelligent and 4. Clever enough to gain access to the library without attracting any undue attention. I rest my case." "Jolly good old boy, replied Alfie sarcastically, but what does it mean?" "Search me matey, I haven't a clue, what does it matter anyway? just throw it in the bin."

"It intrigues me Lee, I'm a historian, I pour over letters and scrolls every day written in Latin or early English, deciphering, decoding, looking for a meaning. The text of this letter is not old, it concerns two people, are they criminals or possible working for MI6, I really need to know, I need an answer."

Leon laughed, "Wow, keep your hair on roomie you're getting a bit carried away, I tell you what, let's stop sitting here like a couple of old fogeys and go and get something to eat and drink, especially a drink OK?" Alfie nodded, "Sounds like a good idea."

It was getting dark outside as Alfie sat on his bed, Leon was out partying as usual. He switched on the bedside lamp then read his tutor's remarks on his latest essay. Something bothered him he reached for the letter from the library and compared the writing it was a match the writer of the letter was Professor Burton. His mind was in turmoil, he kept looking from one document to the other. Unable to sleep he waited for Leon to return; he needed a second opinion.

The bedroom door opened slowly, and Leon entered. "My God you're still awake." "Yes, I need your opinion on something." Leon sat down.

"If it's anything to do with that letter you can forget it." "Please Lee it will only take a minute." Lee sighed, "OK OK, ask me." Alfie showed him the handwriting, "What do you think?" Leon looked carefully then handed them back, "They're identical, written by the same person, can we drop it now?" He ignored the request , "It's my tutor, Professor Burton." Leon held his head in his hands for a minute then spoke, so what Al, so what, you're becoming obsessed about that bloody letter. the whole thing could just be a game between two people, harmless fun, so drop it mate or we are going to fall out – big time." Alfie stared at him for a moment, "It's not you is it, the other person?" "For God's sake, listen to yourself, I've had enough." Lee stormed out of the room slamming the door on his way out.

Alfie woke up the following morning at around 7am, he looked across at Lee who was fast asleep. After washing and shaving he headed for the canteen for breakfast. Over egg on toast, he thought about recent events, perhaps Lee was right I should just throw the sodding letter in the bin and forget about it, but I can't.

He chatted to a couple of friends then headed for the library. He flicked through the Latin translation book in case there was another letter, there wasn't. He decided his next move must be to search his tutor's study for an explanation of starfish.

Leon got up at 8am, he felt bad about arguing with Alfie. After some breakfast he visited the library and sat down opposite Alfie, "I guessed you would be here, he coughed, look Al I'm sorry about last night." "No Lee, it's my fault, you're right I should just drop it, he offered his hand, friends?" They shook hands. Lee looked at his watch, "I've got a couple of days off so I'm off to visit the mater and pater, right got a train to catch, see you soon.

Alton Manor was a large, detached house in north London, Lee pushed open one of the wrought iron gates and walked towards the front door.

He rang the bell and waited. Robbins, the butler opened the door and smiled when he saw Lee. "Ah, an unscheduled visit, Master Beyer, so nice to see you." Leon stepped inside, "Are they in?" Robbins took his coat, "Yes sir, your father is in his study and Mrs Beyer is in the garden."

"Tell dear old Papa I'm in the kitchen." "Very good Sir." As he made his way he wondered if any other people had to make an appointment to visit their parents. The Cook was obviously pleased to see him, "What a nice surprise Master Leon." "Drop all that Master stuff it's just Leon and you're Maggie," he said as he gave her a big hug.

She made him a cup of coffee and they chatted. When Jacob Beyer entered the kitchen Maggie immediately went back to work.

"Nice to see you Leon, is there a problem?" "No Pops, just thought it would be nice to catch up." "Jolly good, let's join mother in the garden. "Oh, Leon how lovely, are you staying long?" "No mother just a couple of days." They made their way to the table and chairs on the lawn.

"How about tea and biscuits everyone?" asked Maria Beyer, before anyone replied Robbins appeared with a tray, "I took the liberty Ma'am." The conversation went very well everyone was relaxed.

Leon always had a strained relationship with his parents. Tessa his older sister was the apple of their eye. She'd got a 1st class degree in law from Oxford and was now a practising Barrister. Father was a retired Judge. They were clearly disappointed that he had ended up at Portsmouth.

The two-day visit went very well, as they stood on the drive about to say goodbye to Leon, Jacob asked to see his railway ticket. Leon was puzzled but handed it over. He tore it up and threw it on the floor saying, "You won't be needing that." Leon was stunned, "I can't stay her any longer, I have to get back to Uni." Jacob laughed as he pressed the 'open' button on the remote control he had behind his back. The double

143

garage door opened to reveal two vehicles, one, the family Bentley and the other a dark blue Range Rover. "This is for you son," he said as he handed over the keys. Leon eyes filled with tears as he turned to his dad and hugged him, "Steady on son, we are chaps you know, he said with a smile, we are proud of you, your mother and I." "Hear hear, shouted Maria, even more so if you graduate."

"Anyway, said Jacob as he looked at his watch, Tempus Fugit son, time you were on your way." They said their farewells and waved as Leon drove away.

Meeting up again after his trip to the Manor Leon told Alfie about his visit and about the car. He was in such high spirits, mainly because his parents did actually care about him. He offered to help Alfie if he was concerned about the letter. He was.

The plan was to wait until the Prof went to lunch then Alfie would search the study while Leon kept watch outside. At noon two days later, as the Professor left the building Alfie sneaked in and made his way to the study, he knocked and walked in. Burton never locked the door as students would often pop in and leave their essays on his desk. He sat at the desk and looked through the drawers that weren't locked, then flicked through Burton's appointments diary, he noticed a recurring item 'Phone K, then a number, he photographed it. Sitting at the desk – something of course he had never done before – he saw what appeared to be two low tables, one on either side, going over to one he pulled off the black velvet cover which revealed two black metal boxes about 2ft square one on top of the other, they were locked, he replaced the cover. Looking at the pictures on the walls he noticed one was a painting of a starfish, lifting it down he turned it over and there stuck on the back was a list of places numbered 1 to 5. Using his mobile again he took a photo then replaced the picture back on the wall. His phone suddenly rang, it was Leon, "Get out, he's back." Alfie rushed to leave the study but to late he bumped into the Prof. "Ah, Alfie Graham, can I help you?"

"Just wanted a quick word Sir, I did wait, but now I'm a bit late for a lunch appointment with a friend, I'll catch up with you later if that's alright?" Burton entered his study then turned to look at Alfie, "No problem, we'll speak soon."

As Leon sat in his car later that evening he thought about the change in his parents, he phoned his sister Tessa and told her about his visit to the Manor and asked her if she had been talking to them. "Well, yes I have, and your name did come up and honestly Al I had no idea they rarely contacted you, I'm always hearing from them by email or phone." "What about the car?" asked Alfie. "What car?" He told her that Pop had given him a Range Rover. "My goodness, I only suggested they should give a small gift to show how much they care about you. But sod the car I'm just really pleased they have told you how proud they are of you. Keep in touch with them, got to go now love, bye."

Leon collected the pizza's and drove back to the Uni. "Ah, the forager returns," said Alfie. While they tucked into their takeaway he handed Leon a copy of the list, he read it aloud. "1.Denbigh Copse. 2.Farthing Field. 3.Milsun Way. 4.Starling Forest and 5 Darnley Hollow, the only thing it tells us is they're all outdoors. Then there's the 4 boxes, how do they fit in?" Alfie's eyes lit up, "Then there's the phone number, it's on the bottom of the list." Leon picked up his mobile and called the number then put the phone down, "It's an antique shop, they're closed, open tomorrow at 9am." "I knew it said Alfie excitedly, they're thieves, after robbing houses of antiques they put them in the boxes then bury them in the ground until the heats off, fait accompli."

Leon nodded his head, "You could be right Al." "Go on then, what's the name of the shop, does it begin with K?" "Right again old bean it's called 'Kenny Gordon Antiques'. "Oh no, please God no," screamed Alfie. "Steady on old chap, what's the problem?" said Leon anxiously. Alfie took a deep breath, "That shop belongs to my sister's new husband."

From an early age Mark Burton had been a fitness fanatic and at 45 he still visits the gym regularly, only now it's a private sports club.

It was 6pm when after a shower he left the club and headed home to his wife Lorna and 13-year-old Joshua. Not long after dinner he was in his study writing what was to be the last letter to Kenny, starfish 5.

Their friendship, or rather their association, started one evening in a pub, both were alone and started chatting and discovered a joint love of antiques. It was later that things changed from friends to business partners. The rules were simple, never to meet except at night, no phone calls unless an emergency and no letters except the library one.

Leon told Alfie to calm down and consider the facts, 1. A strange letter in a book written by your tutor. 2. He and your brother-in-law know each other and 3, there is no evidence of criminal activity. Alfie agreed with the findings but then asked, "What shall I do now?" "Well, next time you see your tutor talk to him about it," replied Leon. Alfie thought for a minute, "But if they are up to something they'll know I'm on to them, he paused, let's have one more look at the book in the library then we're done – agreed?" Leon agreed.

The following morning at 11.30 Alfie entered the library, he went over to the bookcase that held the Latin translation book, with shaking hands he opened it and flicked through the pages. There was a letter. He replaced the book then sat down by one of the tables and read the letter, it said: *Final letter, starfish 5, Friday midnight – Gustav.*

Later that day Alfie showed the letter to Leon who asked what he planned to do. "Well today is Wednesday so on Friday at 11.30pm you and I are going to visit starfish 5 – Darnley Hollow – in your lovely new car and if we see them dancing round the trees naked, we'll know it's all just a game, what do you say?" Leon laughed, "OK, let's do it."

Darnley Hollow was a large uneven field with clumps of bushes dotted around and surrounded by popular trees. About a hundred years ago it was owned by Seth Darnley but now belongs to Dirk Walters owner of Swallow Farm.

The friends parked the car out of sight but close to the field, they took up a position between the trees and used binoculars to survey the area. They were lucky there was a full moon in a cloudless sky. Ten minutes later they heard a car approaching the other side of the field, then another. Two men appeared from between the trees, one was carrying a metal box. Alfie gulped as the men walked toward him, but they stopped by a small bush and pulled it up, it wasn't growing there just pinned down. They dug the earth away then pulled a plastic bag out of the hole and put it into the box. With a handle on either side, they carried the box back towards the trees and out of sight. The sound of the cars leaving broke the silence.

Leon, using his mobile, filmed the whole incident. "We've got them now, said Alfie, I think we should speak to my brother-in-law, Kenny." "We?" replied Leon. "Well, yes, I don't want to go to his antique shop on my own, safety in numbers you know." "Let's go home Al, we'll talk about it tomorrow."

When Kenny and Mark reached their cars, they loaded the box into Kenny's Audi. "I'll call you at the shop tomorrow, said Mark, don't forget we'll use the burner phones." The men shook hands, "Now that starfish is complete, said Kenny, we are going to be a quite well-off couple of chaps are we not?" "Yes, we are," replied Mark.

The shop door pinged as they entered. Kenny was placing some Dresden figures into an oak cabinet, "Hallo Al, nice to see you, who's this?" "My friend Leon, this is not a social call, is there somewhere we can talk?" Kenny went to the shop door and turned the 'open' sign round. "Yes, come into the office." The three men sat down, Alfie spoke first, "I've always liked you Ken, but you have let me and my sister down." Kenny smiled, "Why are you talking like me dad?" "It's not funny, you're a criminal, a thief, a robber." Kenny started fidgeting, "I have to make a phone call." As he took the mobile out of his pocket Alfie grabbed it out of his hand and handed it to Leon.

He examined it, "It's a burner Al." "Oh, so you're the police now, are you? said Kenny, I am NOT a criminal." Then Leon spoke up, "So why are you digging up loot in the middle of the night?"

With his elbows on the table Kenny put his head in his hands. "OK, I'll tell you the truth, me and my friend Mark Burton are coinshooters and certainly not nighthawks." Leon and Alfie looked at each other then at Kenny, "What the hell are you talking about? asked Alfie.

Kenny took a deep breath, "Right, I'll explain, Mark and I are metal detectorists, we look for coins only, nighthawks are illegal detectorists that only work at night, we work at night in order to avoid gawkers, that's people to love to watch detectorists, are you with me so far?" The two friends nodded, "Fascinating, said Alfie, but what about the starfish list and the letter in the book?"

Kenny went on to explain how Mark, using a map of the local area, marked out the five best possible sites worth looking at. When he drew a line from each one to the university it resembled a starfish, so he numbered them accordingly. He approached the owners of the five sites and got signed permission to detect there sharing, of course, the profit, if any, with them. The whole enterprise had to be completely secret. If we were seen to be successful at any of the sites then others would be following in our footsteps and the poor old owners would be inundated with detectorists digging up their fields, hence our night-time activities. We surveyed the five sites then stopped; we were successful with four of them. We would wait a while then legally declare the coins as treasure then sell and no one would ever know where we had been.

"It all makes sense now, said Alfie, I am so sorry I misjudged you Ken, can you forgive me?" "Of course I can, just for a while there to think

I was considered an arch criminal gave me a frisson of excitement." "Thank you Ken, you won't mention it to Glenda, will you?" He smiled,

"Of course not, but incidentally she does know all the facts as does Mark's wife, of course they were sworn to secrecy.

"Just as a matter of interest, asked Leon, but what sort of profit are you looking at, if you don't mind me asking?" "Not at all, actually one of our finds, a collection of Anglo-Saxon coins from the 9th century is worth approximately £500,000, extremely rare you see, anyway lads I'm rather busy so if you wouldn't mind…" Alfie and Leon stood up, "No, of course not, we'll be on our way and once again thank you for being so forgiving." They all shook hands; the lads then left the shop.

About a week later Alfie got a call from his sister Glenda. "Hi Al, I have some good news to tell you, I know I should have mentioned it before but I'm expecting a baby girl." "That's brilliant news, is it too early to be thinking about names?" "Well, Kenny wants to name her Stella."

"That's a lovely name, any special reason?" Glenda laughed, "The word starfish in Italian is Stella Marina."

◆◇◆

Milton Keynes UK
Ingram Content Group UK Ltd.
UKHW022030081223
434064UK00006B/89